Her Secret Amish Child

Cheryl Williford

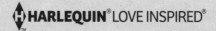

HARLEQUIN® LOVE INSPIRED®

Recycling programs
for this product may
not exist in your area.

LOVE INSPIRED BOOKS

ISBN-13: 978-0-373-89920-3

Her Secret Amish Child

www.Harlequin.com

Printed in U.S.A.

"I appreciate your help, but I can clean the rest myself," Lizbeth assured him.

One of the ladies tossed him a new trash bag. He squatted and began to work on the pile of trash under the steps. "This is my fault," he said, glancing up and grinning at her in the goofy way he had when he was a boy. The memory made her heart skip a beat.

"But I made the mess." She picked up a half-eaten apple off the step and tossed it into the bag.

Fredrik's grin spread into a full-blown smile. "Ya, but I was supposed to fix that raised nail this morning before it could cause someone trouble."

The past fell away and she was a girl of seventeen again, looking into the sparkling blue eyes of the young Fredrik Lapp. He continued to hold her gaze. She pulled her eyes away. The man was having too much fun at her expense. She didn't have a clue what to do about it or the emotions churning in her stomach. But she knew she couldn't let herself grow too close to him. Not this time. Too much was at stake.

Cheryl Williford and her veteran husband, Henry, live in South Texas, where they've raised three children, numerous foster children, alongside a menagerie of rescued cats, dogs and hamsters. Her love for writing began in a literature class, and now her characters keep her grabbing for paper and pen. She is a member of her local ACFW and CWA chapters, and is a seamstress, watercolorist and loving grandmother. Her website is cherylwilliford.com.

Books by Cheryl Williford

Love Inspired

Pinecraft Homecomings
Her Secret Amish Child

The Amish Widow's Secret
The Amish Midwife's Courtship

Fear not, for I *am* with you; Be not dismayed,
for I *am* your God. I will strengthen you,
Yes, I will help you, I will uphold you
with My righteous right hand.
—*Isaiah* 41:10

I dedicate this book to my husband, Henry, who endures endless hours of backstory and plot. To my two daughters, Barbara and Susan. You make me want to succeed. And to God, who gave me writing when I needed a clear and untroubled path. God bless ACFW's Golden Girls critique group. Nanci, Liz, Shannon and Jan…you dear, talented ladies make my job so much easier.

Chapter One

Pinecraft, Florida—a midsummer afternoon

Had she made yet another mistake?

"Don't touch that seat again," Lizbeth Mullet said, stretching across her son's extended legs to wedge their carry-on bag in front of his small brown shoes, hoping to block his incessant movement.

Three times in the past hour Benuel had slapped or kicked at her when she'd scolded him. Each time she hadn't known what to do, how to change the overactive four-year-old boy's behavior. She knew what she wanted to do, what felt like the right thing to do, but her built-in insecurities held her back, forced her to doubt her abilities as a single parent. A torturous night without sleep and little to eat added to her misery.

"Pinecraft, Florida," the bus driver announced. With the flick of his wrist he turned the bus's steering wheel and headed off the highway to his designated stop.

Several people milled around the parking lot of the Pinecraft Tourist Church, waiting for loved ones to arrive. With her father running late, no one would be waiting for her and the boy. They'd left Ohio in secret, telling no one except her father they were leaving or where they were going. There would be no going back. Her late husband's family could not hurt them now.

The Amish and Mennonite people scattered throughout the Pioneer Trails bus began to reach under seats for bags and wake up sleeping children.

Memories of the quaint little resort town she once called home beckoned. Pinecraft Park was on her right, and her father's prosperous chicken farm a few miles down the road, on the outskirts of the small town of Sarasota. She had grown up in this community of Old and New Order Amish people. This is where she belonged. *Gott* willing, she would heal and regain her strength here, around the people who knew her best and loved her.

Scrambling to gather up their belongings while trying to keep Benuel from climbing over her legs and escaping, Lizbeth tucked his bag of toys under her arm and scooped up their satchel from the floor.

"I want my car," he demanded, grabbing for the toy sack.

Standing, Lizbeth put out her hand and forced a smile she didn't feel. "Not now, *soh*. When your *Grossdaddi* comes for us I'll find it for you."

"I'm thirsty." Tall like her and lightly dotted with ginger freckles across his nose, he allowed her to take his hand after a moment of debate and shuffled by her side to the front of the bus. He touched each seat as he passed, counting aloud. "One, two, three."

"That's very good," Lizbeth encouraged. Early on Benuel had showed signs of being slow with numbers and letters. Perhaps his developmental delay had been caused by the long, painful labor she'd endured, but she noticed he'd come out of his shell some since her husband Jonah's death and was beginning to respond to her positive encouragement.

Taking the bus driver's extended hand, Lizbeth stepped down into the sultry heat of the cloudless summer day. She had missed the smell of the sea.

Benuel hopped down each step. His eyes darted around, the enthusiasm in them making her grin. He'd spent too many hours on the farm and was seldom with children his age. Seeing only her husband's family had left him shy and unsocial and sometimes angry, but today he looked different, ready to conquer the world.

"Do you have more bags on the bus, ma'am?"

Lizbeth nodded and let go of Benuel's hand as she dug through her purse for the silver ticket she'd been given when she'd relinquished their larger suitcase back in Ohio. Blond hairs escaping from her crushed prayer *kapp* blew around her face. "Yes. A small one, but I'd like to pick it up a bit later when my *daed* arrives, if that's all right. He warned me he'd be running late."

"Sure. You hold on to that ticket and come get it inside the church when you're ready." He tipped his head. "Thanks for riding Pioneer Trails."

She turned to make sure Benuel was at her side, found him gone and held back a groan. He was nowhere to be seen. Twisting back and forth, she searched the remaining cluster of people standing close by and then saw movement near a row of picturesque shops on her right. Her heart began to pound against her breastbone. It was Benuel, and he was running.

Forgetting to breathe, she chased after him, her black lace-up shoes slapping hard against the hot pavement. Fear pushed her forward. She had to catch him before he made it to the street and oncoming traffic. He had no fear of roads. His experience with the small-town streets of Iris, Ohio, could be counted on one hand. Someone had always been holding on to him, directing his path. But not now.

"Benuel James, stop!"

Startled by her shout, a swarm of shiny black grackles took flight and made their way to treetops across the street.

She quickly crossed the shop's parking lot and pushed off the curb, fear building and twisting her stomach into knots. She couldn't lose Benuel, too.

Her son rushed on, laughing, his reddish-blond hair blowing in the breeze, blissfully unaware of the danger he was in.

Crossing the road, Benuel's body mere inches from her grasp, she glanced both ways as she sprinted close behind him.

Sunrays reflected off the silver scooter approaching. Her heart skipped a beat, uncertain she could reach Benuel before it was too late. She ignored the blast of the scooter's horn and lunged forward, desperate to reach her son before the speeding scooter. Bent forward, she stumbled, but managed to grasp the back of Benuel's shirt as she went down.

Dread grabbed her by the throat. Hot, sticky air filled her lungs as she gasped for breath.

Please, Gott, *please. Don't let us be hit.* She pulled his squirming body close to hers and rolled.

The whirr of the scooter's motor and the screeching of the tires braking caused Lizbeth's body to tense. She held tight to her son and squeezed her eyes closed.

The raw sounds of scraping metal enveloped them and then stopped.

The fast-paced beat of her heart hammered in her ears, her chest, ticking off the seconds.

Close by, birds squawked high in the trees lining the road, and then all was silent.

What had happened?

Afraid to look, she slowly opened her eyes.

Heat shimmered off the deserted two-lane road where they lay. She scrambled up and searched her son's body for injuries.

A startled expression widened Benuel's sky blue eyes. She hugged him close and whispered, "You're fine. Don't be frightened, *soh.*" He seemed unharmed, with the exception of an insignificant graze on his left elbow, no doubt caused from being pulled down on the hot asphalt.

Her breath came fast. She had to force herself to calm down. The boy didn't need to see her fear. He'd had enough trauma in his young life. He was her only living child and so precious to her. What if *Gott* had snatched him away, too? How would she have lived?

She placed him on his feet and watched for signs of pain, but saw none. Relieved, she crushed him to her and cooed as if he were a baby. "My sweet boy. *Mamm* loves you."

"You're hurting me," Benuel squealed, the flat of his hands pushing her away.

Lizbeth sighed with relief. She was upset. Not her son. It had been an adventure to him. "I'm sorry, *liebling.* I didn't mean to squish you." She forced a smile, tried to look normal.

The midday sun beat down on them, penetrating her starched white *kapp.* Sweat beaded on her upper lip. The wrecked scooter had to be somewhere close by.

She grabbed Benuel's wrist and urged him out of harm's way, to the side of the road where a ragged palm tree's fronds rustled in the breeze.

A few feet away, a row of blossoming bushes nestled against sturdy privacy fencing. She scanned under them, and then along the curb where several cars and adult tricycles were parked. The silver scooter had to be nearby. *I know what I heard.*

But there was nothing. No scooter. No rider.

"Look at that man, *Mamm*," Benuel said. "He's sleeping on the ground."

Lizbeth glanced in the direction her son pointed. "Oh, no." Hidden behind a parked car, a ginger-haired man dressed in traditional Amish clothes and black boots lay sprawled across the sidewalk a few yards away. The silver scooter teetered on its side a foot from him, its back wheel still spinning.

Benuel's hand clasped firmly in hers, she hurried over, pausing long enough to instruct her son in a trembling voice, "You stay right here."

His bottom lip puckered. "But I want to see."

Releasing his hand, she said, "I know you do, but stay put, please." Dreading what she might see, she fell to her knees in front of the man's prostrate body and gave him a quick once-over, searching for twisted limbs and blood. He groaned and then stirred, his single status clearly stated by his clean-shaven chin that scraped the rough sidewalk as his head turned in her direction. Dirt and grit smudged his face and neck.

Why is there no one left on the street? I need help, Gott.

"Lie still. You may have broken something," she instructed.

His hand moved and then his arm. Blue

eyes—so like her son's—opened to slits. He blinked at her. A shaggy brow arched in question. Full, well-shaped lips moved, but no words came out.

She leaned back in surprise. She knew this face as well as she knew her own. The man on the ground was Fredrik Lapp, her brother's childhood friend. The last man in Pinecraft she wanted to see. "Are you all right?" she asked, bending close.

His coloring looked normal enough, but she knew nothing about broken bones or head trauma. She looked down the length of his body. His clothes were dirty, but seemed intact.

The last time she'd seen him she'd been a skinny girl of nineteen, and he'd been a wiry young man of twenty-three, with shaggy auburn hair and blue eyes the color of a summer sky. Unbaptized and not yet a member of the church, he'd had an unruliness about him, a restlessness that kept his *mamm* and *daed* worried for his future, and the rumor mill turning with tales of his latest wild escapades.

Now he was a fully matured man, with a thick neck and neatly trimmed hair, cut in a traditional Amish style to his ears. A man who could rip her life apart if he learned about the secret she'd kept all these years.

She leaned in and eyed his clean-shaven

chin. *Why is he still unwed and living in Pinecraft?* There were no significant scrapes on his face, with the exception of a small cut above his left eyebrow.

The sidewalk under him had to be uncomfortably hot. She jerked a length of attached quilt squares from her bag and squatted, carefully slipping the soft folds under his head.

He coughed several times and scowled as he drew in a deep breath.

"Do you hurt anywhere?" Lizbeth used her clean handkerchief to wipe away the blood slowly oozing from the small cut above his left eye.

"Ouch!" He twisted his head out of her reach.

She jerked her hand away and rose. "I thought the blood might blur your vision."

"Is the *kinner* all right?" Fredrik's voice sounded deeper and raspier than it had years ago. He coughed, and with a grunt braced himself with his arms and struggled into a sitting position.

Lizbeth glanced Benuel's way. He was looking at them, his young face pinched with concern. Her heart ached for the intense, worried child.

"*Ya*, he's fine," she assured him, and tried to hold Fredrik down as he started to move about. "Please don't get up. Let me get some help first.

You might have really hurt yourself." He had no family left in the area. *Why had he come back?*

He ignored her direction and rose to his feet, dusting the long legs of his dark trousers down, and then bent to pick her fabric off the ground. He handed her the bundle after doing his best to refold the length of colorful cotton squares. "I got the wind knocked out of me, that's all." He laughed.

He peered at his bleeding arm, shrugged his broad shoulders and rotated his neck as she'd seen him do a hundred times as a boy.

"That was a foolish thing you did," he muttered, his brow arched.

"What was?" she asked, mesmerized by the way his muscles bulged along his freckled arm. It had to be wonderful to be strong and afraid of nothing.

He gestured toward the boy. "Letting your *soh* run wild like that? He could have been killed. Why didn't you hold his hand while you crossed the road?"

She took exception to Fredrik's sharp tone, the disapproving expression on his face. The knot in her stomach tightened and grew. She pushed the ribbon of her prayer *kapp* away and then wiped sweat from her top lip, her frustration growing. She may not know how to properly raise an energetic, belligerent boy, but she was learning and doing the best she could. How dare he chastise her like Jonah and his family had done so many times? "I know we could all have been killed."

Her face grew warm. If only she had been more careful, grabbed Benuel's hand as soon as she'd handed over the ticket to the bus driver. She knew what the boy was like lately. Acting out, not listening to anyone. She looked toward the curb. Benuel's head was turned away, no doubt watching the birds peck away at bugs in the short tufts of grass a few feet away.

With a grunt of frustration, she stuffed the bloodied handkerchief back into her apron pocket and dusted down her skirt. She hadn't been back in Pinecraft a full hour and already was involved in a situation with Fredrik. She had plans for the money she had on her, like paying for somewhere to live. If Fredrik blamed Benuel for the crash, repairing the scooter could leave her totally dependent on her father, and she could not allow that to happen.

"You'll need someone to come get you." She pointed at the crumpled machine on the ground. "It looks like that *Englischer* contraption of yours is ruined." Fredrik had always been a risk taker, never considering the cost to himself or those around him. She knew Benuel was equally to blame for the accident, but it would be just like Fredrik to blame someone else for his share of the mishap.

Fredrik's brows furrowed as he shoved his hand though his disheveled hair. He dropped his arm with a grimace. "That *Englischer* contraption, as you call it, was an expensive scooter. I saved for a year. Bought it less than an hour ago."

Lizbeth swallowed hard. She ran her hands down her arms, her nerves sending tremors through her body, no doubt her reaction to their near miss.

She twisted back toward the scooter. She knew all about men's "big boy" toys, thanks to her Amish *daed*, who prized all things with wheels and gears. This man was cut from similar cloth, but he lacked her father's love of *familye* and commitment to this small community. No doubt he had once again set aside his Amish beliefs to fulfill some foolhardy need for speed.

"I was on my way to the insurance company," he grunted. He turned his broad back on her.

She watched him glance down the empty road shimmering with watery mirages.

He spoke to the sultry air around him. "I thought...what can happen? The insurance office is only a few blocks down the road. What a *bensel* I am."

"It's not insured then?" She stepped back, waited for his reply while gulping down a knot the size of her fist.

He turned back to her, his brow furrowed. "*Nee*, not insured."

Fredrik Lapp didn't know whether to laugh or cry at his own stupidity, not that he wasn't used to making rash decisions that managed to put him in a bad light. He should have made a call from the bike shop, gotten the scooter insured before he left the showroom. But no, he didn't want to be late for work and disappoint Mose Fischer, his boss, who firmly believed in punctuality. *And look what a mess I'm in now.*

With a glance, he calculated the damage to the scooter. The front tire looked flat, the frame slightly bent, the fender folded back where it had hit the metal street pole. No telling what kind of scratches dug into the underside of the machine when it hit the ground.

He groaned aloud, but not from pain. The fancy front light he'd been so excited about, and special ordered, now hung suspended in the air by a single black wire. He'd be out hundreds of dollars for restoration and the scooter's odometer didn't read a mile.

He looked over at the ginger-haired boy with freckles across his button nose and instantly felt contrite, regretting his immature, self-centered thoughts. The boy looked to be young, maybe five or six. Fredrik's heart flip-flopped, the rhythm of the beat kicking up as he realized he might have killed the *kinner* with his carelessness. But the boy had been at fault, too. He should have been holding his mother's hand.

The boy's mother, a tall willowy woman dressed in mourning black, stood next to the child, her protective arm around her son's thin shoulders. *She's protecting him from me.* He silently asked *Gott* for forgiveness. He could have taken a life.

The woman's arched brow told him she didn't believe she and her son had caused the accident, even though she hadn't uttered a single word of accusation toward him. She didn't have to. He knew he'd also made an error in judgment and driven too fast.

Instead of enjoying the exhilaration of speed, he should have been watching the traffic more closely, paying attention to what he was doing. This was no golf cart or three-wheeled bike. He had no experience on a scooter. No idea how to control the metal machine.

Perhaps this was *Gott*'s punishment for him buying such a fancy scooter in the first place. The idea of fast, dependable transportation had made all the sense in the world while looking at the showroom's catalog a year ago. "I'm sorry. I don't know your name," he said, glancing at the widow.

"Mullet. Lizbeth Mullet. And this is Benuel." She nodded briskly, her thin fingers nervously rubbing the side of her son's neck.

Her crooked *kapp* had bobbed on her blond head when she nodded. There were laugh lines etched in her cheeks, but no smile appeared today. He realized she looked slightly familiar, like someone he should know, but he couldn't place her. A lot of snowbirds and Plain people visited the tourist town of Pinecraft, even during the summer months, but she could easily be someone he'd been introduced to at church or met at work.

He glanced over at the fidgeting, serious-faced child and then back to the woman. Sweat curled the fine hairs at the nape of her neck.

Not sure what to do, he extended his hand to her. "My name's Fredrik Lapp. I hope I didn't scare you too much." At first he thought she would ignore his gesture, but then her hand was placed in his. It was soft and looked fragile, even though she wasn't a diminutive woman and stood nearly as tall as him. He felt the power of her grasp, the hidden strength in her, but she was trembling and he was to blame.

An arrow of pain shot through his shoulder and he winced. As she held his gaze, one perfectly arched brow lifted. She inspected his face with probing eyes the color of his *mamm*'s blue-violet periwinkles. A pretty woman, he realized. Someone who would fit fine on his list of women to step out with—if he seriously decided to look for a *fraa*.

Her frown deepened. "Are you certain-sure you're fine?" she asked. "You've gone all washed out. Perhaps you should go to the hospital, be checked by an *Englisch* doctor. I've heard a person can have brain damage and not know it until it's too late."

"*Nee*, it wasn't my head that hit," he said with a laugh and rubbed his shoulder like a child might. "The scooter's front bumper took the impact. I just got the wind knocked out of me when I landed."

"Even so, shouldn't the police be called? It was an accident, and they'll want you to make a report, or do whatever is required."

Fredrik considered her words. He probably should, even though calling would probably cost him a traffic ticket. "*Ya*, you're right. I'll call them now." He gestured toward a café's front door and motioned her forward. "Come in with me. It's too hot to be standing on the sidewalk. I don't know about you, but a glass of sweet tea sure sounds *gut* to me."

Chapter Two

Inside, the café pulsed with life. The lunch crowd of local Amish and Mennonite folks, with some summer tourists sprinkled in, blended into a loud, but happy, sea of faces.

Still shaking, Lizbeth followed a waitress in and ushered Benuel into the small booth upholstered in cheap red leather. Fredrik flopped down across from them a few moments later, making himself comfortable as he ordered a glass of tea and one of the cook's famous sweet rolls.

"What would you two like? Sweet tea, a Coke?"

"We'll have ice water, *danki*," she answered, watching Fredrik's face. She searched for and found the bump on his nose. She'd caused the break when she'd thrown a basketball at him years ago.

She relaxed. He still didn't seem to recognize her, but there was no reason he would. She'd been dishwater blond as a teen, and full of life. Nothing like the rake-thin, ordinary, mouse-blond woman she'd become, with her unremarkable face that drew no second glances.

"Can I have Coke?" Benuel blurted out.

She gave her son a warning look. He shouldn't be asking for treats. Not after running off. Unsure, she fought an inner battle, trying to decide whether to be hard on the troubled child and not knowing when to hold firm to her convictions. She hadn't been allowed to discipline Benuel in any way while her husband was alive. He or his mother always stepped in, took control of the boy. Punished him for her mistakes.

Benuel's hopeful expression vanished. His forehead took on a sulky frown. She reached to pull him closer, but he pushed away with a grunt of annoyance.

"My treat," Fredrik offered.

She looked across the table at Fredrik. His grin was easygoing, relaxed. "*Danki*, but *nee*. He has to learn to obey."

Fredrik made a face at the boy, his nose crinkling up in a comical way. Benuel giggled slightly and then ducked his head. Silence had been a firm rule enforced by Jonah and his parents back in Ohio. Children should be seen and seldom heard. Especially *her* child.

Lizbeth watched the all-too-familiar lift of Fredrik's brow, the way his lips curved as he laughed at Benuel's reaction to his teasing. His smile revealed a tiny chip on his front tooth. He'd fallen his last summer in Pinecraft. He'd chased her, trying to get his straw hat from her hand, and slipped on wet stones.

"How about some pancakes with strawberries? They're my favorite. Come on, *Mamm*. Let the boy enjoy life."

He had no idea the inner conflict she endured, the indecisiveness she fought regarding Benuel's discipline. Her reply came out harsher than she intended. "I *am* letting the boy enjoy life. Benuel's being disciplined for running away and can't have sweets right now. He'll be having plain food for the rest of the day as his punishment."

The bell over the café door rang. Lizbeth glanced over and then jumped up, rushing into her father's waiting arms.

"I've been looking all over for you, girl," John Schwarts scolded, but gave his daughter another tight hug that spoke of his love for her. "You should have waited at the church. I told you I'd be a bit late."

"I'm sorry, *Daed*. It got so hot. We came in

for a quick cold drink of water." She looked at Fredrik over her father's shoulder and saw a glimmer of recognition in his eyes. He finally knew who she was. *Something to worry about later*, she thought, lowering her gaze.

Her cheek nuzzled against her father's barrowed chest as she listened to the sound of him breathing, the beat of his heart. It had been five long years since she'd left the safety of his arms. It was good to be home.

"It's no matter," he responded, as he slid in beside Fredrik. "So, what are you doing here? I thought Mose told me you were working early today."

Fredrik had the decency to look a little embarrassed. He glanced over at Lizbeth.

She gently shook her head, praying he wouldn't say anything about their near accident. She already had Fredrik thinking she was a bad *mamm*. She didn't need her *daed* thinking it, too.

"I was…ah…am working early today. I just thought I'd stop and get a cold glass of tea first," Fredrik stammered, pulling his summer hat off and setting it on his lap. "Lizbeth was kind enough to share a booth with me. It's pretty busy in here."

The waitress hurried over and interrupted the men's chatter. Lizbeth took a deep, calming breath. Her *daed* looked good. His new wife, Ulla, must have been taking fine care of him.

John smiled his grandson's way. "So this is Benuel. How are you, *soh*?"

Benuel frowned and then looked away, all the while tapping his fingers on the table. "I'm not allowed to speak to strangers," he muttered.

Lizbeth patted her *daed*'s hand. "He'll warm up. It'll just take him a while."

"*Ya*, sure. I understand. You were always a bit standoffish with strangers at his age. We'll get to know each other at the chicken farm, won't we, Benuel?"

Benuel ducked his head, his ginger-colored hair falling in his eyes as he nodded slightly.

Fredrik spoke up, ending the awkward moment. "You going to work at the church tomorrow, John?"

"Certain-sure, I am. That roof's leaking like a sieve when it rains."

Lizbeth took the glass of water handed to her by the waitress, slid Benuel's water to him and watched her father's face light up as he talked about future church repairs with Fredrik.

It was so good to be back home. Her *daed* had changed very little. Oh, he'd gotten some grayer, a bit more round at the middle, but he looked happy.

Benuel kicked her leg under the table. She

flinched. "Drink your water, and keep your legs under you," she instructed, warning him with her eyes.

"He's as fidgety as those new roosters I bought." John laughed.

Lizbeth tried to act normal. Her father didn't understand, didn't know about Benuel's medical issues yet. She realized she'd have to tell him about the boy's ADHD issues, but now wasn't the time, not with Fredrik Lapp sitting there, listening to every word said. "He's a hyper young man, that's for sure," she said and pushed Benuel's water closer to him. She hoped she'd never have to tell her *daed* about the things she and the boy had seen and been through while in Ohio.

Benuel swished his hand across the table, knocking over the water glass. He smirked Lizbeth's way, rebellion written across his young face. "I'm sorry," he said, righting the glass as cold water and chips of ice streamed into her lap.

Fredrik watched Lizbeth's face redden, saw the way her hands shook as she grabbed napkins to sop up the spill. He still couldn't believe this woman was the Little Lizzy he'd grown up with. She'd changed. And here she was, back in town, with a rowdy little boy. Her son had knocked over the glass on purpose. Fredrik was sure of it, and he could tell John knew it, too. The older man's forehead was creased into an irritated scowl. Turning his head, he looked at the *kinner* closely. Benuel's expression had become calm again, almost serene. As if nothing had happened.

That boy needed a talking-to, but Fredrik could tell by the look on Lizbeth's face that she wasn't going to discipline him in front of his grandfather the first time they met. She'd leave it for another time. Poor woman looked exhausted and frazzled from her long trip home.

Fredrik grabbed the napkin under his water and helped Lizbeth clean up the mess. "Kids always seem to manage to spill their water," he reassured her with a smile.

"Ya," she muttered, picking up the last of the ice cubes scattered across the table. Her face still flushed with embarrassment. *"Danki,* Fredrik."

She looked at her father, her fingers twisting the wet napkin in her hand.

Fredrik watched the tiny blue vein in her neck pulse with tension.

"Benuel is often overactive, *Daed*," she said, glancing at Benuel squirming in his seat. "But he's a *gut* boy."

"Ya, I know he is," John said, nodding. His

smile was that of a patient grandfather who understood the ways of rambunctious boys.

Lizbeth visibly relaxed, her lips turning up at the ends. "I'm so glad to be home. Benuel needs a strong man like you in his life."

"*Ya*, well. You've got the whole town of Pinecraft at your disposal, *dochder*. We'll all pitch in. You're not alone."

Tears glistened in her eyes as she put her arm around her son and pulled him close. "I'm so glad, *Daed*. Change can be hard for Benuel. All he's ever known is the farm. Life's been difficult for him."

John smiled gently. His big calloused hand patted hers. "I'll go and grab your bag from the church. You can wait here until I get back." She handed a ticket to John and he nodded at Fredrik. "Don't be too late to work," he said with a smile.

Fredrik shook John's hand. "I'll see *you* tomorrow at the church. Make sure you wear your loose pants. The ladies are cooking for us."

John nodded. "I'll be there." And he walked to the door.

Fredrik turned back to Lizbeth and saw a slight smile on her face. "It's been years, and I know I've changed," she said, "but I'm assuming you've remembered me by now, Fredrik. I'm Little Lizzy, Saul's *schweschder*."

Fredrik leaned toward her with a grin. "Of course I know who you are. I realized it as soon as you greeted your *daed*. Little Lizzy. I can't believe it. I'd heard you had married and had moved away while I was in Lancaster. Why didn't you tell me who you were as soon as we met?"

She shrugged her shoulders. "It didn't seem important. And I wanted to see how long it would take for you to remember. I knew it was you the minute I saw that ginger hair of yours and your broken nose."

He trailed his finger down the bridge, to the almost invisible bump, thinking of that day so many years ago. "*Ya*, and I remember who broke that nose. You had a mean pitching arm back then."

"I still do."

Fredrik glanced up and saw one of Sarasota's finest walk through the café door, the gun on his hip standing out in the crowd of Plain people and tourists. "The police officer is here. I've got to go. It was good to see you again, Lizbeth." He stood and pulled her to his side in a hug, his arm sliding around her slim waist.

Then he let her go and walked off, peeking over his shoulder at her one last time. She'd been the picture of calm since her father arrived. Her *daed* was what she needed. A strong man to lean on.

He walked toward the police officer, his heartbeat kicking up. He'd leave Lizbeth and the boy out of this situation. She had enough on her plate. Going by the shake of her head earlier, she wouldn't want to talk to the police right now anyway, not when her father could return at any moment. Could she have thought Benuel was at fault for the accident? If she did, she was mistaken. He knew he was to blame and would make sure the police knew it, too.

Chapter Three

The next morning, Ulla Schwarts glanced at the quilt top Lizbeth had been working on since sunrise, and smiled. "You've only been home a day and that top is almost finished." Bent at the waist, she swished a sudsy dishcloth across the big wooden farm table, reaching for and finding a spot of dried plum jelly that needed scrubbing. "You sew pretty fast."

"*Ya*, it came together quickly," Lizbeth agreed, looking up from her breakfast, over to her father and then his wife of one month. She smiled as the gray-haired woman wiped sweat from her forehead with the back of her hand, and then went back to cleaning the big wooden table positioned in the middle of her *mamm*'s well-loved kitchen.

Lizbeth already liked the spirited older Amish woman and found merit in her humor and work ethic. It would take some time to adjust to seeing another woman in her mother's *haus*, caring for her *daed*, even though years had passed since her *mamm*'s sudden passing.

"It's time I go check on the chickens," her father stated, then wiped egg off his mouth. His chair scraped the floor as he rose. He lightly kissed Lizbeth on the forehead. "I'm so glad you're back," he said for the hundredth time that morning.

Lizbeth smiled, joy warming her heart. "Me, too, *Daed*."

"You have any plans for today?" he asked.

"Nothing important," Lizbeth muttered, and grinned. She'd had a hard morning with Benuel and didn't have much energy left in her.

"I'm off then." John kissed his wife's cheek and whispered something in her ear that had her giggling as she swatted him out the back door with her dishcloth.

Still smiling, Ulla commented to Lizbeth, "There's a sewing circle that meets at the civic hall on Tuesday mornings if you have a mind to go." Ulla shoved a stubby water glass into the sea of dishwater and swished a cloth around in it.

Lizbeth gathered up her plate, coffee cup and the remains of her half-eaten bacon and eggs destined for the chickens' scrap bowl. "Does Berta King still go?"

Ulla shook her head and moved to clean the stove. "Not since the cancer took hold."

Lizbeth paused, her hand going to her heart. "I didn't know." The spry little woman had taught her to quilt and had been her mother's best friend and confidante for more years than she could remember. Berta had been there to wave her off when she'd quickly married and left Pinecraft five years before.

"*Nee*, you wouldn't, would you? Living so far away. I only see her when I take meals over on Tuesday and Friday nights. She looks bad. So thin and frail. Abram's not looking so good himself, poor man. Someone told me their daughter from Ohio is coming on the bus. She'll help out until her *mamm* passes, and then take her *daed* home with her."

"It's never *gut* to be alone." Lizbeth adjusted the work scarf on her head and then plunged her hands into the sink of hot soapy water. The water burned a small scrape caused by her fall in the street the day before.

She began scrubbing dried egg yolk off her plate. She had to find a way to make Benuel understand that roads were dangerous. Living in a busy tourist town held hazards he didn't understand at such a young age. It would take time and patience to guide him.

Perhaps she clung to him too tightly now that she had him all to herself. Benuel had always been easily distracted, but he had grown more willful of late, even cruel at times. She remembered the kick he'd given her under the booth the day before and sighed deeply. He needed a man's firm hand, but the thought of marrying again sent her pulse racing wild with fear. Not that any man in his right mind would want her as his *fraa* once he found out she was emotionally damaged.

And the last time she had married for her child's sake hadn't gone so well. What would she do if anyone discovered the truth about Benuel? It would ruin both of them.

There had to be another way to help him grow into a strong man without a father in his life. Perhaps settling down near her *daed* and the kind people of Pinecraft *would* bring about the stability he needed, as her father had suggested. At least she prayed that it would.

Ulla plugged in a portable electric fan and positioned it on the long wooden counter nearest her. "You'll need this if you're going to wash those breakfast dishes. The humidity is high. We must be expecting a storm."

"Danki," Lizbeth muttered and plunged in another yolk-covered plate.

Ulla hummed as she shuffled across the room, a stack of folded towels in her arms.

A glance out the kitchen window revealed threatening gray clouds. A gust of wind twisted two small palm trees to the ground.

The old German clock in the living room ticked away the remaining minutes of the morning. She rinsed her hands and rehung the dish towel on its wooden peg next to the window and then pressed her hands into the small of her back. A long, busy day stretched out in front of her and she had no energy left.

She had to talk to Benuel about his behavior at the breakfast table, and was dreading it. He'd poured milk on Ulla's clean tablecloth. He'd done it on purpose, even though her father claimed it had been an accident. All she seemed to do was scold the child, when all she wanted was to pull him onto her lap and hold him until his anger went away.

"So, you have nothing planned for your day?" Ulla came back into the room with a load of sheets ready to be washed. Her tone and smile were friendly and inviting, unlike the daily dramatic scenes that played out back in Ohio with her mother-in-law. She could never please the woman, no matter how hard she tried. And she had tried.

Lizbeth took in a deep, cleansing breath, her memories of Ohio pushed to the darkest recesses of her mind once more. She smiled. "I've got the usual. Keeping Benuel entertained and getting that quilt top finished after I make our beds."

Ulla paused under the kitchen's arched door. She braced a wicker basket, fluffy with unfolded sheets, against her stomach. "We have church service tomorrow. I make it a practice to help with the cooking of the communal meal. You can join me if you like. It would give you a chance to get reacquainted with some of the ladies of the community."

Preparing the communal meal had been one of Lizbeth's mother's favorite chores. Being one of the volunteer church cooks was something Lizbeth could embrace now that she was back, not that she was a very good cook. Going along with Ulla would give Benuel a chance to play with children his own age. But doubt stalled her. "I don't know. He's such a handful today."

"*Ach*, don't let his acting up stop you from doing a good deed. You haven't met Beatrice, my oldest *kinskind* yet." Ulla laughed, her smile animating her wrinkled face with a glow. "Now that child is a certain-sure handful. She and her sister Mercy will be there." The woman's tone became serious. "Benuel needs the company of other *kinner*, Lizbeth."

Lizbeth's face flushed. He needed so much more than she seemed able to give him, but she would learn. "*Ya*, maybe I will come after all."

"*Gut.* I'll get this load of sheets folded and then we'll make a list for our trip to the store. I thought I'd make chicken and dumplings and a peanut butter shoofly pie. Is there anything special you'd like to make?"

Benuel had smashed his fist into the center of the last cake she'd baked, sending chunks of chocolate cake all over her mother-in-law's kitchen floor. "Maybe I'll make chocolate cupcakes for the *kinner*. Chocolate is Benuel's favorite."

Ulla laughed. "Beatrice and I have an understanding when it comes to cupcakes of any flavor. She behaves and does what I tell her, or I get to eat hers. You might try that on Benuel. Missing a few cupcakes might bring about a bit of good behavior from the boy."

Lizbeth found herself smiling. "*Ya*, I might try that. *Danki*." Her smile grew. "You've been so kind to us since we arrived, Ulla. I want to thank you for opening your home, taking us in."

"Nonsense. This is your home, too. John and

I are happy you moved back to Pinecraft, sudden or not." Ulla set the basket on the floor. "Having you here has been a blessing. But what's this John tells me about you already looking for a home of your own?"

"*Ya*, I am looking, not that you both haven't made us feel so very *willkumm*. It's just that Benuel needs to settle into a routine before school begins." Still so unsure of her parenting skills, she wasn't positive she would be putting him in school. She had to decide soon, but not today.

Ulla grinned as she flipped out a square tablecloth and shoved it into the washer. "I own an empty house that's up for sale and begging for a family to bring it back to life. It's simple and *Amisch* Plain, but not too far from here and close to the Christian school. If the local man who asked about it doesn't buy it, you're welcome to rent it until you marry again. We have a busy weekend, but John can show it to you on Monday."

"That would be *wunderbaar*. A simple house would be an answer to prayer," Lizbeth said, ignoring Ulla's comment about a new marriage. She had no intention of marrying again. It would be just her and Benuel from now on.

Surely the money she had squirreled away would be enough to make rent payments until she could find a part-time job and someone safe to leave Benuel with. Maybe there would be enough left over for a few pieces of second-hand furniture. When they had left Ohio, she had taken nothing but their clothes and a few of Benuel's favorite toys. She pushed away her reasons for leaving the farm, unwilling to bring back the harsh memories that haunted her un-guarded sleep each night.

Gott's will be done. He had brought them back to Pinecraft, to the Plain people she'd grown up with, and she was grateful to be home.

At noon on Monday, Fredrik leaned his old bike against an orange tree and turned on his heel, ready to begin his search for a wife in the crowd of Amish women standing around, chatting.

After seeing Lizbeth Mullet wearing a pretty blue dress at church the day before, and hear-ing two pastors preach on the joys of married life, he'd lost sleep that night, tossing and turn-ing, but managed to make a firm decision. It *was* time to forget Bette, who had accepted his proposal and then run off and wed his best friend in Lancaster County, where Fredrik was completing his apprenticeship. He would buy Ulla's house and settle down. It shouldn't be too hard to find someone to marry him. Perhaps Lizbeth Mullet would consider him and if not her, someone else just as comely. Whoever he chose, though, would have to understand that theirs would be only a friendly partnership. An attempt at showing the community—and himself—that he could grow and become responsible. He'd never give another woman his heart after the way Bette had stomped on it.

The woman he married would have to be patient, accept him as he was. He wasn't exactly sure how much he could change his youthful ways, but almost killing a child had affected him deeply. It was past time he stopped behaving like a *youngie* and got on with his life.

He ambled across the dry park grass, over to the food tables and joined his boss, Mose. The square-shouldered Amish man greeted him with a nod of his head and then filled one side of his sturdy paper plate with fried chicken. He inched his way forward, toward a bowl of hot potato salad decorated with perfect slices of boiled eggs and olives.

"You're late. You almost missed out on my Sarah's specialty," Mose said, adding an extra helping of the creamy potatoes to his too-full plate. "It's almost gone."

"I see that," Fredrik smiled and took the last

of the potato salad with a half-moon of boiled egg buried on top.

"You oversleep?"

Fredrik cleared his throat before speaking. "No, I had to pay a traffic ticket. No insurance."

Glancing back, Mose said, "Is this one of your yarns?"

Fredrik glanced up. "*Nee*, I'm not joking."

"Then what do you mean? The police don't give tickets for bike riding."

Fredrik lumbered close behind Mose, both men still circling around the table laden with food. "I wasn't exactly riding a bike." He reached across the table for three meaty ribs shining with barbecue sauce. He added a forkful of pickles as an afterthought and then speared a meaty chicken leg covered in crispy fried batter.

Together they headed for the drinks table, and stood in a line with community leaders and hardworking Plain men waiting for a cold glass of sweet tea. The big oak tree draped with moss spared them the bright overhead sun.

Fredrik had hoped to speak privately with Mose, but the park grounds were already packed with people supporting the lunch that would bring in enough money to pay for the new roof on the church.

Fredrik frowned, not liking the idea of someone from the congregation overhearing what a fool he'd been. In Pinecraft, simple situations were known to grow into full-blown gossip sessions, innocent words passed on from family to family until the truth could barely be recognized.

Balancing his tall glass of tea and a few napkins against his chest, Fredrik followed close behind Mose.

"What were you riding, a golf cart?"

"No, a scooter." He waited for the critical remark he knew was coming. Acting as his mentor and older brother, Mose had warned him about leaning too close to *Englischer* ways, but Fredrik had prayed about buying the scooter and *Gott* had remained silent. Fredrik had taken His silence as approval, and he'd been wrong.

"Were you speeding?" Mose's brow arched as he placed his glass of tea on a cloth-covered picnic table and slid his plate in front of it.

Fredrik joined him at the table and smiled at Sarah, Mose's *fraa*, as she kissed her husband fondly on the forehead, then hurried off, pushing a twin stroller of chubby *kinner*. A curly-haired toddler followed her, tugging at the back of her skirt. "Sarah's looking well rested. The twins must be sleeping through the night at last."

The big blond-haired man wasn't smiling.

"Don't change the subject. You'll have to tell me sometime. Are you hiding a secret about this scooter you borrowed?"

"I didn't borrow the scooter. It's mine. I picked it up the other day. That's why I was late to work." Fredrik took a gulp of tea and sat the sweating glass back on the table.

"*Ya*, well. You said you were buying one with your savings, but didn't you know you'd need insurance for the thing?"

Fredrik nodded. "I did know, but I got ticketed before I could get the insurance." He paused to pray silently over his food and then shoveled in a mouthful of potato salad and chewed as he thought back to the day of the accident. An image of the pretty widow came back to haunt him. If only he could get her and her son off his mind. He pictured them round-eyed with worried looks. Were they still traumatized by his stupidity? He hoped not.

"Well, it makes me to wonder if you should have prayed more about this magnificent piece of machinery of yours," Mose said after he'd prayed. "Perhaps *Gott* isn't pleased with your purchase and is letting you tie a rope around your neck." Mose flashed a sardonic smile that showed a piece of mustard green stuck to the front of his tooth. The man bent forward and went back to attacking his food.

"*Ya*, you might be right." Fredrik nodded. "Nothing *gut* has come from the purchase." The other side of their picnic table was still empty. Now was as good a time as any to speak to Mose. He blurted out the lines he had practiced. "You think there's any chance I could get a church loan for a down payment on Ulla's house?"

Mose laid down his fork. "*Ya*, sure. We have money set aside for such as this. Ulla's house would make a fine house for a young man like yourself. There's plenty of room for a *fraa* and *kinner*." He smiled, probably expecting his words to unsettle the unmarried man. "I'm sure she'll sell it to you. She has no use for it now. Let's walk over by the river and talk for a moment."

Throwing his paper plate into the trash for the flies to buzz around, Fredrik ambled alongside Mose, his mind racing.

Houses in Pinecraft seldom came up for sale since they were usually passed on from family member to family member. When they were put on the market, they were too dear for most young people. Perhaps Mose could convince Ulla to sell the house to him at a reasonable price.

"So, you're finally ready to marry," Mose

said, stopping to sit at an old picnic table close to the river.

Fredrik followed his lead and sat. *"Ya."* He'd never experienced being tongue-tied in his life, but it seemed he couldn't get his words to untangle on his tongue to form a complete sentence. "I…" he said and hiccupped from a nervous stomach. He groaned silently and then plunged on, forcing the words out. "Before we talk about the loan, I need to tell you I had an accident on the scooter the first day it was mine." There! The words were out.

"My *daed* used to talk to me about his *bruder*, Thomas. Seems all his life my *onkel* liked all things fast. The *Englisch* ways appealed to him more than *Gott* and the church." Mose waved at his small blond son running past on short, dimpled knees.

Fredrik watched clusters of Amish and Mennonite people eating their meal. A cooling breeze blew across the park. Tablecloth edges flapped in the breeze like white sails at sea. A gull's sharp cry rang out overhead, perhaps predicting doom and gloom for Fredrik's project.

He got a quick glimpse of Lizbeth Mullet and Benuel sitting with a crowd of women one table over. Today she was smiling and talking to her son in an animated way, the wind blowing lengths of her fine blond hair around the simple neckline of her yellow dress. Regret tightened his stomach once again.

"Church and *Gott* mean a lot to me. More than that scooter," Fredrik said, and swallowed hard. "I'll be thirty soon. It's time I settle down and get married."

"Have you found anyone suitable?"

"I've made a list of available women in the area." He laughed and glanced back at Lizbeth, wishing she was someone he could mention as a prospective *fraa*. "Ulla's sister is a matchmaker, and coming for a visit soon. If I can't decide on someone, I hope she'll help me find a woman from the surrounding communities while she's here."

"Have you considered Lizbeth Mullet? She's widowed now and could use a husband to help raise her *soh*."

Fredrik wanted to admit he was considering her, but he had a feeling she'd never agree to stepping out with him. She just thought of him as her big brother's annoying friend. "Not really, but I will add her name to my list. Nothing ventured, nothing gained," he said with a smile. "Who knows? *Gott* might speak to her about me." A home and wife was what he needed, but could he find the right bride without allowing his heart to be broken again? He hoped so.

Chapter Four

Later that afternoon, Lizbeth hoisted the heavy green garbage bag out of the industrial-size plastic container and hastily placed it on the church's tiled kitchen floor. It was heavier than she'd anticipated, and made bulky by several plastic milk jugs she'd added to the jumble after making chocolate pudding. She tied the bag off, and with a grunt of determination, gathered her strength, lifted the burden and wrestled it to the back door.

Twisting, she turned the knob and hip bumped the sticking door open. Sunlight and a cool breeze poured into the sweltering kitchen.

Five narrow steps and a four-foot drop greeted her. *Great! Just what I need. More obstacles in my path.*

She glanced around and found a row of enormous black trash cans lined along the church. They were at least six feet away.

Six feet or six inches, she was going to get the trash into one of those cans if it took her the rest of the afternoon. Stubbornness fed her resolve. *I can do this.*

Positioned on the second step, her back to the yard, she heaved the plastic bag up and then dropped it on the top stair.

"You need help with that?" a masculine voice asked from somewhere behind her. She recognized it was Fredrik.

"*Nee*, but *danki.*" She shot a glance over her shoulder. Fredrik was bareheaded and wiping sweat from his brow with a colorful bandana.

"You sure?"

Doubt rang in his words and spurred her on. As a girl she'd had no defenses against his teasing, but infatuation didn't rob her of her voice now. "*Ya*, I'm sure. Go about your business, Fredrik. I can manage." Somewhere in her mind she knew she probably should accept the man's offer of help, but she shut out the voice of reason. She'd been controlled too many years, her choices taken away from her. This was her project. She had something to prove to herself. She'd get the bag of trash into one of the cans if it was the last thing she did.

With another grunt, she stepped down, lifted

the oversize green bag and repositioned it on the second step. She heard Fredrik's muffled snicker and tensed. Her shoulders came back and her backbone went rigid. With trembling fingers, she straightened her work scarf, took a deep breath and prepared for the next step. She might not be as strong as the muscular man standing behind her, but she had determination that would carry her through to the end.

She grabbed hold of the bag, stepped down, her foot finding the edge of the narrow step.

Her stomach tightened into a knot as she swayed, fought to regain her balance and repositioned her foot. With another grunt, she jerked the bag up. It caught on the edge of the step and puckered. She tugged carefully. The slit formed and then grew. The bottom of the bag gave way with a rush.

There was no time to jerk her feet away. Trash covered her legs and the toes of her black shoes with a goopy mixture of tomato sauce and coffee grinds. Potato peels and an assortment of empty plastic containers fell through the stairs onto the dirt.

Lizbeth glared down between the stair's wooden slats to the growing heap of trash. Her *mamm*'s gentle words of reprimand echoed through her mind. *Pride is a sin, child. It will only bring you misery.*

"Here, let me help you with that." Fredrik came into view.

She noticed the ends of his ginger hair curled attractively around his light blue shirt collar. He was covered in sawdust and small wood chips. A smudge of roof tar told her he'd been working with the roofing crew she and the other ladies cooked for.

He reached for the bag, his hand covering the gash at the bottom as he eased it away from her.

She released her hold, not wanting his touch, and watched the muscles in his forearm bulge as he raised her burden as if it were weightless. She slipped him the fresh bag she had tucked in her apron pocket and watched as he lifted the trash can lid and chucked the bag in, wiping his hands down the front legs of his pants as he gave her a satisfied grin.

She stamped her feet against the wooden step, dislodging most of the coffee grounds from her shoe, but red sauce splotched her legs.

Heat suffused her face as she looked up and noticed the last of the kitchen staff standing in the open doorway, all smiles and giggles, watching her exchange with Fredrik with great interest.

Lizbeth cringed. Every time she turned around she was causing herself some kind of embarrassment, and somehow Fredrik always managed to be involved. "*Danki*. I appreciate your help, but I can clean the rest myself," she assured him.

One of the ladies tossed him a new trash bag. He squatted and began to work on the pile of trash under the steps. "This is my fault," he said, glancing up and grinning at her in the goofy way he had when he was a boy. The memory made her heart skip a beat.

"But I made the mess." She picked up a half-eaten apple off the step and tossed it into the bag.

Fredrik's grin spread into a full-blown smile. "*Ya*, but I was supposed to fix that raised nail this morning before it could cause someone trouble."

The past fell away and she was a girl of seventeen again, looking into the sparkling blue eyes of the young Fredrik Lapp. He continued to hold her gaze. She pulled her eyes away. The man was having too much fun at her expense. She didn't have a clue what to do about it or the ripple of emotions churning in her stomach. But she knew she couldn't let herself grow too close to him. Not this time. Too much was at stake.

An hour later Fredrik and six other men sat at the square table in the corner of the kitchen. Lizbeth refilled each man's glass with cold milk, accepted their thanks and then busied herself with the last of the pots and pans.

She listened to the deep hum of their conversation, not to eavesdrop, but to enjoy the sound of men talking in a friendly manner. She'd spent too much time alone on the farm in Ohio. And the only conversations she'd heard when her husband and his family were around had been harsh and ugly. She'd used the time to gather her thoughts and make life-changing decisions. Jonah's sudden death allowed her to act on her choices.

Memories of Jonah filled her mind. Lean, with plain, unremarkable features, he had been the only man she'd stepped out with after Fredrik had left Pinecraft without a word of goodbye. Always kind and gentle, Jonah's love for her had been evident in the way he'd talked to her and showed her respect at the start. And he'd been one of the few who knew the truth, knew of her sin. She'd thought he'd be willing to treat Benuel as his own son. But she'd been wrong. About everything.

In Ohio, where his family farmed, she'd found herself embedded in a hostile community of rigid Old Order Amish rules. The people lived bitter lives. The painful memories of Benuel's birth followed quickly by news of her mother's sudden death had put a fresh sting of unshed tears in her eyes.

After his birth, Benuel was taken from her and given to Jonah's mother, who'd just lost her youngest boy in a farming accident. Jonah had longed for sons of his own, children who would work the family farm with him in his later years.

And when Lizbeth got pregnant again, she'd thought he'd get his wish. But the babies died a few moments after their birth, born too early to survive. Jonah grew impatient with her as the years passed. She could still feel the sting of his words after their deaths. *Where are my sohs? You carry them in your stomach, but they die, gasping for air. What have I done to earn this punishment? You have brought sin into my home. Their deaths are your fault.*

Deep inside, she knew Jonah was at fault for the loss of her twin sons. When he drank, his physical abuse had cost her much too much.

Lizbeth shoved a chocolate chip cookie loaded with walnuts into her mouth, eating out of taut nerves and not pleasure. She had to remind herself Jonah would never hurt her or Benuel again.

She submerged an oversize saucepan into the hot dishwater and began to scrub. Once again she relived the sound of the accident that took her husband's life. The terrible screech of tires, the scream of their horse.

Visions of the overturned buggy, the *Englischers'* car mangled and burning next to it. Her breath grew ragged. The terrible sights and sounds of that night were seared deeply into her memory. Jonah had been badly burned, his chest crushed by the weight of their dead horse. She could still see the sterile white hospital room where he later died, his suffering finally over. She'd disappointed him in every way imaginable.

The police later confirmed her suspicions. Her husband had been driving drunk the night of the accident, and their old mare, Rosie, was out of control and running wild when the *Englischers'* car hit the buggy.

She'd been too ashamed to admit she knew he had taken to drink to dull the pain of his lost sons. Jonah had lashed out at her earlier that dreadful night at the supper table. He'd screamed at her, told her she was useless. But she knew it had been the drink talking and she had forgiven him everything he'd said. Who could blame a man whose *fraa* could not give him more sons? Benuel had been a witness to the wreck, to her moments of insanity.

She glanced down at her trembling hands, at her little finger, once broken and now permanently twisted out of shape. A reminder of Jonah's fits of rage when her tiny boys were laid to rest in the cold ground. Dark memories surrounded her like a heavy shawl. She pushed the memories away and went back to work, her thoughts on Benuel. He mattered now. No one else.

The final pan scrubbed and rinsed, she placed it on a dish towel and leaned against the stainless steel sink, her eyes closed, pushing away all the misery, the memories of her past life with Jonah.

Her son had paid the highest price of all. He had no *daed* to follow around, no man to emulate, to show him how to grow strong. And it was her fault. She knew she had to do something. He needed a father, but she didn't want another husband, someone she would disappoint. No Amish man in his right mind would want a traumatized woman with the built-in ability to fail. Gott*'s will be done in Benuel's life*.

The scrape of a chair behind her caused her to turn. Fredrik moved toward the commercial-size refrigerator, his empty glass in hand. The other server had left the room moments before, leaving her alone with the last shift of workers. She jerked a square of paper towel from the roll and dried her hands. "Can I get you something?"

He stopped, turned toward her with a warm smile. "You're busy. I can pour my own milk."

"Would you like some ice in it?"

He quietly observed her. "Little Lizzy, I can't believe you remember I like ice in my milk."

"I'm the one who introduced you to it." She narrowed her eyes at him. "And I'm not so little anymore. Neither one of us is, Freddie."

"I still see your *bruder* as often as I can. I'm sure *he* still thinks of you as little."

Lizbeth found herself smiling at the mention of her older brother. "*Ya*. His two boys look just like him, ain't so?"

Fredrik nodded. "Remember those childish fights we used to get into? You were always such a pesky kid, hanging around, bothering us. Back then, Saul and I were convinced you were only born to annoy us."

He laughed again and Lizbeth felt her face and neck flush pink with warmth. When she was little, both boys had made it clear they didn't want her tagging along. Her young life had been full of merciless teasing. "*Mamm* made Saul take me along. I didn't want to go." Her mother's image impressed itself on her mind. The beloved woman had been tall and always too lean. She'd worn simple dresses of cotton made by her own hands. Lizbeth could almost hear her *mamm*'s words floating in the air around her. Ya, *Saul. You will take Lizbeth with you, or you won't go yourself.*

She gently edged her memories of her mother away, along with the pain of her loss. "*Mamm* always wanted me out from under her feet so she could clean or quilt with the ladies." She wiped at the side of the big fridge and opened the door, her thoughts back to her youth as she wiped down the rack where milk had been spilled. Her childhood feelings for the man standing next to her flushed her face warm again. She felt eleven years old again, longing for Fredrik to take notice of her. Embarrassment had her chatting again. "You boys teased me terrible when you took me fishing. You threatened to use me as bait."

"*Ya*, because you didn't know how to shut up." He softened his words with a lopsided grin. "You were so skinny back then. I was always afraid you'd fall in the river and we'd have to fish you out."

She stood tall, almost eye to eye with him. With a mind of its own, her finger poked at his broad chest. "*Ya*, well. I never fell in and you didn't have to save me once." She snickered. This was one of the few times her above-average height served her well.

"Nee." He stepped back and removed his hand from her arm. "I never did have to save you, but you ran off lots of fish."

She took the glass from his hand, splashed in frothy milk from a cold metal pitcher and then dropped two ice cubes into the milky swirl. "Two enough?" she asked, looking up at him.

He had a strange expression on his face and was smiling like someone who had just been given a special Christmas gift. *"Ya.* Sure. Two is perfect," he said and turned away with the glass of milk in hand, but not before winking at her with one bright blue eye lined with rusty brown lashes.

She turned on her heel and left the room, but not before turning back and giving the man one last look. He sat down at the kitchen table circled with men and went back to eating like nothing had happened.

She hurried away from the kitchen, leaving the men to fend for themselves. She'd left Benuel alone with the other children a long time. It was best she checked up on him and made sure he was behaving himself. Left to his own devices, there was no telling what he'd get up to.

She forced her thoughts to Benuel and off Fredrik. What foolishness. The man had never been drawn to her.

Chapter Five

Lizbeth leaned her borrowed bike next to her father's big-seated tricycle and followed him up the steps of the porch. She was encouraged the two of them had finally found spare time to look at the empty house together.

The street was quiet, the homes well kept. The front lawn was neatly cut and edged. Made of white clapboard, with a brown tiled roof, Ulla's house looked exactly like every other home in the small Amish community. Plain and nondescript as it had been described to her. The dwelling had a big wraparound porch, graced by two oversize cushioned rockers. They made the home more inviting, an added bonus she hadn't expected but was thrilled to see.

Her foot on the last step, she glanced back at the neighborhood, trying to take it all in at once. She turned back to the white house and admired the tidy beds of fragrant pink rose-bushes nestled along each side of the porch. The wood fence surrounding the backyard had a pleasant gray patina and looked strong enough to hold her son behind its sturdy walls.

She smiled as she went up the steps, picturing Benuel climbing trees and running around in the privacy of his own yard, where he'd be safe from the dangers of the road. This house would suit them to perfection if the inside was as nice as the outside.

Her *daed* turned the key and stepped back so Lizbeth could precede him. "*Ya*, well. Like I told you. There's a few repairs to be done. The roof needs a shingle or two, but all that will be fixed before you move in."

The entry hall was clean and spacious, the hardwood floors shining from a fresh coat of beeswax. He led the way to the great room filled with comfortable-looking furniture. Solid navy drapes were pulled back at each side of the big windows. "You'll get the morning sun in here."

"*Gut,*" Lizbeth said, hoping to find a brick fireplace and then realizing she wouldn't need one in Florida. There'd be no more snow or icy roads to contend with. No more shivering in buggies, carting wood and milking cows. She smiled and continued to follow her father.

Across the entry hall he led her into a big square kitchen. The walls were lined with wooden cabinets painted a glossy white. A large *Englischer* stove and refrigerator sat across from each other. The sunny kitchen window, framed with pale blue checkered curtains, crowned the deep country sink in front of her.

"Ulla kept a small table and chairs placed by the door, but her daughter wanted them since her *daed* had made them. I'm sure you can get a set for a fair price at one of the auctions coming up."

Lizbeth imagined a round table with four chairs in the empty floor space and grinned. "Perhaps I can get Mose Fischer to make me one."

"*Ya*, he could make it fit perfectly in here. He's known for the quality of his work." Her father ran his hand down the length of the kitchen's work-top counter and smiled. "I'm sure Ulla and her daughters had many good times here, baking and making memories."

"Perhaps renting the house to me isn't a good idea. It could be difficult for her."

"*Ya*, well, not that hard. She said she took her memories with her when we married. She seemed happy to move in to my home. This phase of her life is over. Her new life has begun, just like yours will when you marry again. Now, let's go look at the bedrooms at the back and see if you think Benuel would be happy in one of them."

"Will she be leaving all the furniture?" Lizbeth ignored her father's comment about her getting married again and ambled toward a beautiful hall table made of oak wood and polished to a high shine. A real beauty. She held her breath as she waited for an answer.

"That's up to the renter." Her *daed* chuckled. "Houses are hard to come by in Pinecraft and most renters want their homes to be furnished, especially if they're snowbirds from up north and only staying a short while each year."

"If I decide to rent the house, I'd want the furniture to remain," Lizbeth assured him and then hurried into the first bedroom off the hall, her excitement building as she examined the good-size room with a double bed and wooden dresser that matched. "I left the farmhouse in Ohio as is and walked away with nothing but our clothes." She could have said more, but didn't. She hadn't told anyone about her life in Ohio. Why share the misery? Speaking out would change nothing in her past and erase none of the damage done to her soul. Her one regret was walking away from the graveyard that held the bodies of her babies.

She would always grieve the two tiny souls.

She'd asked *Gott* to protect them from Jonah's bruising blows. But *Gott* chose a different path for them. Both had died in her arms. It had been *Gott*'s will, but she would never understand. She'd left a part of her heart there in that cold Ohio soil. She would never forget her boys.

Fredrik moved fast through the spacious apartment behind the house on Ulla's property—*his* property—noting the discolored walls begged for a lick of paint. He frowned as he walked into the kitchen and viewed the table. Once sturdy, it now made do on three legs and threatened to fall. It would have to be thrown out and a new one built. Someday he would be building furniture for his home, maybe even a cradle for his firstborn son.

He rubbed his hands together as he visualized the new eating area. He would build the replacement table a bit bigger than this tiny one.

He opened a door at the back of the kitchen. Narrow shelves lined the shallow pantry walls, ready for jars of homemade jams and spices.

He turned on his heel and looked back into the kitchen. He could picture someone in the galley-shaped work space, cooking their simple meals. He took in a long, satisfying breath of air. Whiffs of gasoline and machine oil wiped the smile off his face. To keep its musky smell from seeping into the apartment, he'd need to seal the walls of the storage shed built against the outer partition of the room.

He glanced out the window to the big white house down the driveway. His spirits rose. He had finally found the home he had been looking for. Ulla's house was certain-sure good enough to bring a *fraa* home to, and he'd been surprised when she'd lowered the price down to a manageable amount for him this morning. He'd start to search for his bride from amongst the church ladies. He'd missed a lot of church services the past three months, his mind busy with work and not on spiritual growth.

He was a little hesitant when conjuring up faces of the eligible women he knew. What if he decided on someone and they turned him down? Without a doubt, he knew Lizbeth Mullet would reject him.

The color of Lizbeth's hair caught his attention, drawing him away from his thoughts. He couldn't settle on her just yet. He would have to grow spiritually, find a way to make himself the kind of man she'd want for a husband, and then see.

Thoughts of marriage were on his mind all the time, filling every moment of the day now that he'd made his decision to wed.

For years the idea of courtship with anyone

set alarm bells ringing. Unrequited love had sent him running back to Pinecraft and the comfort of a small, lonely apartment in Sarasota. He'd finally healed, but he hadn't been ready for this step of faith. Until now.

He didn't know what had changed, but something was building in him, an excitement, some emotion he didn't completely understand. Perhaps it came because of the loneliness he endured, or the way his body ached when he worked extrahard for nothing more than his own benefit. Both were reminders that he wasn't a boy anymore. At twenty-nine he wasn't exactly long in the tooth, but time was passing and he wanted to find someone to share his life with. Maybe even start a family now that he had a family home to raise *kinner* in.

He heard voices and made his way to the open apartment door. Chicken John stood on the side steps of the house Fredrik had just purchased, his back to him, talking to someone inside.

"There's a work shed outside, not that you'll need one. But the backyard is perfect for Benuel." Chicken John stepped down onto the driveway.

From inside the house a feminine voice called out, "*Gut.* I'll be right out."

Fredrik walked into the bright sunshine, leaving the apartment door ajar.

Chicken John placed a hand against his brow, shielding his eyes from the bright sunlight. A smile of welcome lifted the corners of his mouth. "You scared the life out of me, Fredrik. I thought we were the only ones on the property. Weren't you supposed to come by yesterday?"

Fredrik returned his smile. "I was, but I got busy at work and ran out of daylight. I hope you don't mind me coming by today."

"*Nee*. Today is *gut*. You know you're always welcome, but I think you might have left it a bit too late if you were interested in buying this house." He leaned toward Fredrik and whispered, "Lizbeth needs a rental house. If she likes what she sees she'll snatch this place away from you."

Nerves gripped his stomach. He'd have to be the one to break the news about the sale of the house to Lizbeth and her father. He hated the idea of slipping the house from her grasp, but he needed it as much as she did. She could always stay at her father's if she didn't find a place to rent. His need was more urgent. He wanted to marry. If he could talk Lizbeth into courting him, she would have this house as her own, and he'd have a wife he might eventually learn to love. If he could find a way to trust her with his heart.

The screen door squealed for oil as Lizbeth appeared and stepped onto the porch. She turned in his direction, her brow furrowing from the bright noontime sun. She wore the same navy dress and shoes she'd worn to church on Sunday. Again today her expression was relaxed and friendly.

"Fredrik," she said and nodded.

He tipped his straw hat in her direction and grinned back, noticing her smile reached her warm blue eyes. "Lizbeth."

"You two have made friends?" Chicken John said, his tone inquisitive.

Fredrik spoke first. "A long time ago—"

"*Ya*, well. Remember, Benuel and I just happened to meet Fredrik at the café and became friends," Lizbeth interjected, cutting off his words. Something in her gaze told Fredrik she still didn't want her *daed* to remember they knew each other as children. "And speaking of Benuel, we really should be on our way. Ulla offered to watch him for a few hours. Not the whole day."

"*Ya*, you're right. We've taken too long," her father agreed. He reached around, locked the doorknob from the inside and then shut the side door behind him. "Good seeing you, Fredrik. I'll call you about the house repairs later today."

"*Ya.* Later today is perfect. I'll be at the shop. It's *gut* seeing you again, Lizbeth. Tell Benuel I said hello."

She dipped her head in acknowledgment. "I'll tell him. You have a pleasant night," she said and hurried away, the sun reflecting strands of gold in her hair.

His heart racing at the sight of her, Fredrik pushed his straw hat down on his head and followed behind them as they crunched down the pea gravel driveway. He was ashamed he hadn't found the nerve to tell Lizbeth he'd bought the house she wanted as her own, but his dreams of working in the leaning shed blossomed. Became bigger than life.

He observed Lizbeth as she gathered up the skirt of her plain blue cotton dress and climbed onto her bike. He liked the way she held her head high, as if nothing could touch her.

Both turned and waved as they pedaled off. He wondered about the widow wearing a different colored dress now. Did that mean she was over her time of mourning? When she'd arrived in Pinecraft she'd still dressed in black.

He knew grief could make a woman distant and unfriendly, but Lizbeth seemed friendlier now. Perhaps he'd done the right thing putting her name on his list of potential women to step out with. The fact she had a boy didn't bother him one bit. It just made his odds better, since she might be looking for a prospective husband to help raise her son. And she might not expect a potential husband to immediately surrender his heart.

He looked back at the simple wood house and lifted his shoulders as he took in a long, contented breath. He or Ulla would tell John he'd bought the house. No doubt the man could find another house for Lizbeth, but until Fredrik found a suitable wife, he was in no hurry. The widow could rent from him and live in the house if she wanted. He didn't mind sharing, but she'd have to move once he married. He truly believed *Gott* would help him find his bride soon.

Fredrik made his way back to the apartment door, his gaze wandering to the backyard shaded by a big oak draped full of hanging moss. Lizbeth's son seemed full of energy. This yard would have been the perfect place for a boy like him to play. It still could be.

Pushing those thoughts aside, he opened the solid wooden apartment door he'd left ajar and stepped back inside, his eyes quickly adjusting to the dim light. The picture window at the side of the big room had a set of closed, wide wooden blinds that blotted out the daylight. He tugged on their dangling cord and stepped back as dust floated on the sunlight flooding the room. The walls had once been a bright white, but now looked yellow with age. Just as he'd thought, they would need to be washed down and painted.

A slow walk back around the apartment's galley kitchen and bathroom told him there were a lot of small jobs to be done, but the bones of the place were sound enough and well worth the price of a few repairs. This place could bring in a good bit of profit if he could get it finished by tourist time.

He opened the only bedroom door and was surprised at how large it was. He could see a full-size bed fitting in the room, and a big dresser. A comfortable chair placed over by the window would be perfect for reading.

The closet door almost fell off its hinges as he opened it wide. Inside, space was limited, but Plain people didn't need lots of space for clothes and shoes. He propped up the closet door and began to tap his pencil against his chin as he wandered back through the rooms, pondering the price of the work needing done in the bathroom as he passed. It might take a while to get a new wall of tiles up, but it would be well worth the effort.

Concentrating on the task at hand, he walked back into the kitchen and pulled out a chair. He'd make a to-do list and hope he'd get the opportunity to restore the apartment back to its original beauty before winter when places rented for a premium. If it came out as good as he thought it would, he may want to increase the amount of rent he'd had in mind.

Living in Pinecraft, instead of his apartment in Sarasota, would bring him closer to work, give him extra time to find the perfect wife. If Lizbeth moved in for a time, he could live in the apartment and keep an eye on her and the boy. A woman living alone with a *kinner* would always need looking out for and he was just the man to do it. A smile creased his face as he wrote down his supply list. That idea of living close to Lizbeth Mullet appealed to him. In fact, the idea of marriage to her appealed even more.

Chapter Six

At dusk the next day, Fredrik lumbered up the house's front steps, the leather soles of his boots squeaking as he made his way across the wooden porch left wet by a sudden summer storm.

Too full from a hot meal at the café, and tired from a long day at the furniture shop, his shoulders sagged as he lugged his heavy toolbox by his side. He longed to go back to his apartment and kick up his feet, but he'd made a promise to himself he'd start the work in the newly acquired house and wasn't backing out. He'd get busy with the list of jobs needing done inside, finish inspecting and making additional plans on the separate apartment at the back of the property, and relax later tonight.

He stumbled over a can of paint and nudged it out of his way, weaving in and out of several other cans he'd left scattered too close to the front door. His thoughts touched on the attractive Amish waitress who'd served him at the local café during his dinner. She was new to Pinecraft and full of questions.

Marriage fresh on his mind, he'd enjoyed her chatter, but Lizbeth Mullet was the only woman he could imagine on his arm. And that had to change. He had no idea what she thought of him, or if she'd even be agreeable to starting a courtship.

He wiped sweat from his forehead with the back of his hand, unlocked the front door and nudged it open with his shoulder.

Inside, the house was quiet. The warm air smelled musty from weeks of being shut tight. He'd need to work fast if he hoped to get through the foot-long list of jobs that needed doing inside the house. Chicken John had spoken with Lizbeth about the sale of the house, and she'd agreed to be Fredrik's tenant for as long as he needed one. She wanted to move in the next day so he knew he must hurry.

He set the toolbox down, opened the windows in the living room and then went back to eyeballing the entry hall's wood trim and walls. He had seen several dings on the outside of the wooden front door that would need seeing to. The dents looked like they'd been there for years, but he saw no good reason to just overlook them. His father had taught him if a job was worth doing, it was worth doing well.

His fingers scrubbed at the fine stubble on his chin as he made a mental note to add wood dap and fine-grit sandpaper to his list of supplies that needed to be picked up.

Fredrik meandered from room to room. He opened doors and looked in all the usual places that received wear and tear.

He made a mental note that the worn linoleum in the front bathroom would need to be switched out. New tiles would spruce the small room up, but would probably take more time than he had. Lizbeth wouldn't want him underfoot once she moved in with her son, but she may have to put up with him being around from time to time. It would be a *gut* opportunity for him to get to know her and the boy.

The bathroom doorknob wiggled in his grasp. One more job on his list. Might as well get to it now. Fredrik made an adjustment and tightened down a few screws and then wiggled the knob again. Done.

He ran the faucets in the sink and tub. All were in good working order.

His mind always raced ahead of the projects at hand. He wondered about the gallons of white paint he had brought with him. The house was smaller than he remembered. He'd probably bought too much, not that he couldn't use the leftovers when he began the apartment remodel at the back of the property. He was in a hurry to finish both projects. He'd decided he would live in the apartment for a few months when his lease ran out at the end of the month, or maybe rent it now, and lease it out during the Christmas holidays, when rentals went for top dollar. Hopefully he'd have enough time to work on his projects on his days off.

He flushed the toilet and waited for the tank to fill. The sound of a crash came from the direction of the kitchen.

He froze midstep, listening.

Posters had been put up at the post office warning that several houses had been broken into recently, ransacked by thieves and then left for the local family to find.

He tiptoed past the toolbox. Soundlessly, he eased out a heavy wrench and moved toward the closed kitchen door. A nonviolent man by belief and custom, he still couldn't stand by and let someone break into the home without trying to stop them.

He raised the wrench high and leaned against the kitchen door while silently twisting the old-fashioned glass doorknob.

On high alert, he peered into the well-lit kitchen. Everything seemed in order.

A cardboard box lay on its side on the floor. The contents, a plastic bottle of bleach and a tight bundle of dust cloths and cleaning brushes, lay scattered around.

The hair on his neck rose. Ulla had said she and Molly would clean the house after he finished with the repairs in a day or two.

Fredrik stepped into the room. His heart skipped a beat as a feminine voice ordered, "Stop, or I'll shoot."

Lizbeth had no weapon, with the exception of the long scrub brush she brandished across her arm like a shotgun. What was she to do? She'd never struck a person, but the brush seemed to have a mind of its own and lifted, poised to strike. Didn't she have a right to defend herself? Would it be so wrong?

She pressed the long-handled brush against her heaving chest. A labyrinth of emotions surged through her as a dark boot and trouser-covered leg stepped into the room.

She'd been warned by Ulla to be cautious when she'd left the house that afternoon. Thieves had been targeting the vacant homes of hardworking Amish families who spent the hot summer months in the north. She should have had her father come with her to check the house.

She whispered a brief prayer and waited for the right moment to strike. With all her might she shoved at the opening door, cringed as she heard it hit something solid and then watched as the booted foot disappeared. Metal clanked against the floor on the other side of the door.

She gulped in air and raced for the back door, only to find she'd blocked her own getaway with the new kitchen table and chairs.

She whirled around, her teeth clenched as she struggled to face the intruder. Her only way out was past the man sprawled on the hallway floor, his head in his hands.

Her heart beat loudly in her ears as she inched closer. There was something familiar about the ginger hair protruding through the man's fingers as he massaged his head. Concern replaced fear. "Fredrik! What are you doing here?" She straightened, her arms thrown open wide in disbelief. "I could have hurt you."

"I'd say you did hurt me." Fredrik raked his hair out of his eyes and frowned up at her as he rubbed his forehead.

"I'm so sorry. I thought you were a burglar. Here, let me help you up." She offered him her hand, but he ignored it.

He winced and rubbed his head again. "I

heard a noise and came to check it out. I see no reason for you to clobber me with the door." He rose with a stagger and used the doorjamb to brace himself. Ginger curls dangled across his flushed forehead.

Guilt-ridden, she grabbed a kitchen chair and shoved it toward him. "Here, please sit." She motioned toward the chair. "I thought you were someone up to no good." She tugged at the prayer *kapp* ribbon dangling against her neck.

He dropped onto the wooden seat of the chair. *"Danki,"* he muttered, his tone none too friendly.

In the past they would have made a joke about all this, laughed and poked fun at each other for being afraid in an empty house. But they weren't children anymore, or misbehaving teens. They were adults. Strangers really. She wasn't sure how he'd react to being pushed to the ground by a swinging door in his own house. "You didn't answer my question. What are you doing here?"

"I told your *daed* I'd be doing some of the repairs in the *haus* this afternoon."

She wiped sweat off her top lip. "Why didn't he tell me? I'd hoped to make preparations for our move tomorrow."

"Your guess is as *gut* as mine. Maybe he thought you'd be finished by now. It is gone seven." He looked toward the kitchen curtains blowing in the wind. "Most *mamms* would be at home, feeding their *kinner* and getting them ready for bed." He glanced around, scowling. "Where is Benuel?"

Was his comment a rebuke? Probably not. She was just being touchy. Benuel was with her father and Ulla, well fed and bathed by now, and waiting for his bedtime story. She owed Fredrik no explanation, but she gave him one anyway. "He's with my *daed*, probably eating the chocolate cupcakes I made earlier and no doubt staying up till all hours while I behave wickedly with my broom and dustrag."

"I didn't mean to imply—"

Out of past frustrations she'd reacted too harshly. "No, I know you didn't. Forgive me. I guess I'm tired." Lizbeth picked up the spilled cleaning utensils scattered across the floor. She glanced back at Fredrik, her grip tightening on the handle of the scrub brush. Feeling threatened moments before, she would have used it on him. The thought disturbed her. Poor man was only doing what he'd promised to do. Getting the house ready for his first tenant.

Lizbeth put away the brush and sat the box of supplies back on the counter. She gave Fredrik a long glance and found he looked remarkably young, his hair tossed from his fall, the freckles on his nose more pronounced under the indoor lighting. But then she noticed the slight bags under his eyes, signs of exhaustion around his mouth. Her mood softened even more.

No doubt the man had worked all day and now was here to work on the house. Had he had time to eat his evening meal? The least she could do was offer him a cold bottle of refreshment. She reached for her carryall and pulled out a sweating bottle of cold apple juice. "Why don't you drink this and then get back to your projects."

He reached for the bottle and downed half with one long pull. *"Danki,"* he said and wiped his mouth with the back of his hand as he rose. He moved to leave the room, but paused just inside the door. "I'm sorry I scared you." His gaze held hers for a long moment, but then he vanished, leaving her alone with her thoughts, though the woodsy fragrance of his soap stayed with her.

Lizbeth busied herself for a few minutes, spraying vinegar on the already-clean windowpanes and wiping them. She scrubbed with all her might and then paused as she heard footsteps coming back toward the front of the house. She waited for Fredrik to reenter the kitchen.

His boots shuffled as he crossed the entry

hall and made his way back to the bedrooms. Without even trying, Fredrik had a way of pulling out memories, making her think of how things used to be when they were young.

She heard a window in the back bedroom open and then close. He was probably checking the caulking. She'd seen slight cracks around several of the windows from the constant Florida heat. No doubt he'd patch where it looked like the rain could get in.

Silence surrounded her. The last of the sunlight coming in through the opened kitchen window waned and disappeared. As she locked the small window over the sink, an outdoor light came on in the neighbor's house, chasing away the beginnings of night shadows and flooding the backyard with a golden hue.

She glanced around the unfamiliar kitchen that was to become hers to use. She compared this warm, welcoming space to the drafty, uninviting farmhouse she'd shared with Jonah, and sighed. One day *Gott* would allow her a measure of peace.

With the cleaning box in her arms, she left the kitchen and made her way into the great room. Two side-by-side windows had been left open. A brisk breeze blew in, fluttering the long drapes hanging at each side of the twin windows. The fragrances of damp foliage and the sea intertwined.

A feeling of melancholy settled over her. She wished she was sharing this house with a man, a husband who would love her and her *soh*. But she knew that was not to be. She'd make do with Benuel's love. He would be enough. Later, after she'd gotten over the painful memories of her first marriage, maybe *Gott* would send someone her way. Someone she could deeply love. Someone who wouldn't judge her for her past mistakes. Once emotionally healed, she'd welcome a kind and gentle husband into her lonely life. But now was too soon. She had things to forget, things that still troubled her dreams.

She pulled the chocolate whoopie pie out of her starched apron and walked slowly down the hall. Squatting in front of the electric socket on the wall, Fredrik used a yellow screwdriver to twist in a screw. She paused, watching him, interested in the way his muscles rippled beneath his shirt and then went taut across his back when he stretched.

She cleared her throat and he shot to his feet. She held out the whoopie pie. "I thought you might have missed your dinner. This might help."

"Danki," he said, reaching out and taking it.

He looked at her in a way that made her stomach clench. His blue eyes had always fascinated her. "I made it myself," she muttered. "I hope you like it."

"I'm certain-sure I will," he said, touching her hand as he reached out.

She couldn't ignore the tingle coursing through her fingers. "I'll be going now. Benuel will want his stories read to him."

"Okay, see you later," he said, pocketing the treat.

She held his gaze. "Don't work too late. You look tired."

"I'll be going soon." As an afterthought, he added, "Would you like me to walk you home? It's getting dark."

"*Nee*, there's no need. I have my bike. *Daed* told you I'll be moving in tomorrow morning, right? I gave him the rent to give you," she asked, watching him, taking in the way the shine from the bedroom's overhead light reflected on his ginger hair, the way his generous smile pressed grooves around his mouth.

"*Ya*, he gave me the money and told me you were eager to get settled. I hope you have a good night," Fredrik said, shoving his hand through his hair and pushing the curls off his forehead.

"*Danki*," Lizbeth whispered and left the

room. She walked briskly out the door and down the walk to her bike, her thoughts on Fredrik Lapp and the man he had become. The thought came to her. Would he make a good husband now? Could he love her? What kind of father would he be? She pushed such foolish thoughts aside and pedaled with all her might toward her father's chicken farm. She'd entertained those thoughts about Fredrik once before. But he'd left, and she'd moved on. What did it matter to her now if he'd make a good partner? She wasn't looking for a husband.

Was she?

Chapter Seven

"Look out! The cat—"

Before Fredrik could react, a streak of gray fur jumped over his booted foot, skittered on the entryway's shiny floor and scampered off toward the back bedrooms.

"Oh, no! Look what you've done now!"

His friendly mood waned. Did she think he purposely let the cat into the house? "I didn't mean—"

"I know. I'm sorry, Fredrik. Forgive me," Lizbeth said, her expression apologetic. "Perhaps you should come back another time, when I'm not so tired and out of sorts."

He witnessed her inward struggle to be civil, saw a nerve tick in her jaw. She smiled, but she didn't look like any ray of sunshine.

Had moving day been that hard on her? All the furniture was in the house and he'd seen

Otto, Chicken John and several sweaty community leaders milling around outside with glasses of sweet tea in their hands. She had plenty of help. And from the tower of boxes lining the entryway, he could see there were lots of donations coming in, everything she'd need to set up the rented house.

Lizbeth was different since returning to Pinecraft. More intense. As a kid she'd been a mild-mannered pest, with more energy than he and her *bruder* could keep up with. She'd kept him laughing with her silly antics. Perhaps marriage hadn't agreed with her, or she had poor health. What had happened to her while she was away in Ohio? None of it was his business, but he still wondered.

Ulla's head poked out of the kitchen door, her face red and sweaty, a frizzy riot of gray curls circling her round face. The edges of her mouth lifted in a slight grin and then she disappeared with a wave.

He rubbed the back of his neck. "Your note on the door said—"

"I know, but you let that cat in and it took me hours to get her out the last time she got in." She cut him a frustrated glance as she raked a dangling curl out of her eyes and shoved it up under her cleaning scarf.

He was frustrated, too. Mornings off were

hard to come by. The shop was usually too busy, or a furniture order had to go out. Mose had called and asked him to deliver a box of linens to Lizbeth's on his way out of work yesterday and he'd forgotten until this morning. Sarah, Mose's wife, was busy with sick children. He'd agreed to tote the box over, even though it was an inconvenience and meant he'd miss an hour of fishing while it was still cool. He'd agreed because he enjoyed Lizbeth's company, liked being around her a lot more than made him comfortable. He could have just as easily claimed to be too busy and let someone else bring the box to her. He slid a guarded look at the overtired widow.

Dark shadows bruised the tender skin under her eyes. He regretted his uncharitable thoughts. This poor woman needed cheering up and he was just the man to do it.

He hid a grin as he noticed a cluster of spiderwebs clinging to the edge of Lizbeth's left eyebrow. It danced around as her frown deepened. As a child she'd hated spiders. If she knew one's web dangled off her face, she'd panic. And he wasn't going to tell her. It would be too much fun to see her reaction when she noticed on her own.

Always ready for a good prank, he cleared

his throat. He held back the full-blown laugh that begged to come out.

She frowned at him, her brows low. "*Ya,* well, I still have to catch that cat again."

He stepped through the threshold with his burden. The perfectly folded stack of sheets and pillowcases smelled of homemade lavender soap and fresh air. "Sarah Fischer sent these yesterday," he said, and presented the box to her. "I forgot to bring them to you."

"*Danki.* Put them there." Lizbeth jabbed her finger toward the floor and then adjusted the cleaning scarf on her head. She unknowingly knocked the dangling cobweb off her brow and onto her wrist. "How am I going to catch that cat? It took me half my tuna sandwich and the patience of Job to run her out last time." She hurried away down the hallway, muttering to herself, "I have no sandwiches left. What am I going to do?"

"Let me help you. It's the least I can do," he offered. He couldn't help himself. He wanted to be around when she found the spider's web and went running through the house, screaming.

She stopped in her tracks and turned, hands back on her hips. "You've done so much already."

"I only—"

"*Ya,* let the animal in." Her shoulders

drooped as soon as her words were out. "Oh, don't listen to me. I'm just not dealing with all this very well." She smiled weakly.

"Look," he said, pointing to the flash of gray that told him the cat was on the move.

They both rushed down the hall. Lizbeth ran into the room and crouched down, searching under an unmade bed. Her headscarf almost fell off in her rush and she positioned it back in place with a pin.

Fredrik joined her on the floor, looked under the bed. Two bright green eyes glowed back at him. "What a pretty kitty," he crooned. "Come close and I'll pet you."

Lizbeth lifted her head, an incredulous expression lingering on her features. Her brow rose. "Don't get friendly—"

"Shush," he hissed, the edge of his mouth lifting in a grin as he shoved his hand under the bed. "Come here, pretty baby. Let me pet you."

"I can't believe—"

"Shush," he repeated. "I know what I'm doing. If you'll just be quiet for a moment, woman, I can solve your problem."

The cat hissed and slapped at him, but its claws weren't extended.

"*Ya*, I can see you're making great strides," Lizbeth said, her mood lightening as she tried to hide a giggle behind her hand. She glanced back under the bed. "Perhaps a broom will encourage her out?"

Fredrik sat and reached low, his hand slipping closer to the cat. "Come on, kitty. You remember me. I gave you a good scratching yesterday."

Her head bobbed back up. Her smile failed her. She scowled. "You encouraged that cat to hang around?" There was an edge to Lizbeth's whisper.

He ignored her for the moment, which was hard to do. She looked beautiful today, her cheeks rosy, her eyes spitting fire from a morning of frustrations. "Come on, kitty. Let me touch you." He bent lower, moving his fingers carefully as the cat whipped its tail back and forth in agitation.

"I'm getting the broom. I don't have time for this," Lizbeth groused and rose to her feet.

He glanced up. The cobweb had moved from her hand to her cleaning scarf. It was just a matter of time now till she found the web. "*Ya*, you get the broom," he said and went back to coaxing the cat out.

The room grew quiet. As soon as Lizbeth was gone, the cat came out of hiding and sauntered toward him, surrendering to the temptation of a neck rub. Fredrik scooped up the ball of fur and scratched it under one ginger-

and-gray ear. Content, it purred. He smiled as Lizbeth hollered in the kitchen. He could hear Ulla's attempt to calm her, but she was having none of it. He chuckled to the cat. "She must have found the cobweb, Purr-Baby. Our work here is done. Time to go fishing."

Lizbeth carried the broom back to the bedroom, her thoughts on Fredrik. She was grateful he'd brought the box of linens. She really was, but why didn't he just go? She had so much to do before nightfall. She had no time for his silly pranks. He had to have seen the spiderweb on her scarf. Ulla saw it quickly enough.

Fredrik knew she'd had a strong aversion to spiders and their webs as a teen. And how dare he shush her like a child? This was *her* home for now. He may be the owner, but she'd paid her rent. He was just there to deliver a box, nothing more. It was time for him to go.

She had more than enough to stress over this morning with her concerns about moving in to the big house. Plus, Benuel had woken in rare form and started the morning off on the wrong foot. She'd never lived alone, and as the local break-ins continued, they fed her feelings of insecurity. She sighed.

It wasn't that she didn't like cats. She did.

She just didn't have time to bother with one right now.

Determination in her every step, she hurried to the back of the house and entered the bedroom, only to stop in amazement. Fredrik stood next to the bed, the cat cozied up in his arms. "Poor little kitty," he said as he glanced at her and then back to the cat, his expression innocent.

"That cat's been nothing but trouble and I want it gone." Lizbeth lowered the broom to the floor.

"This little darling is looking for a place to have her babies, that's all. She doesn't mean to be a bother." Fredrik lounged back against the wall.

Lizbeth's heart dropped. "Babies?" Her eyes widened. "That pregnant cat is not staying here. I have enough to do, plus I have to find a job once we're settled." A frown creased her forehead.

Fredrik beamed across the room at her. "You might want to reconsider your decision about keeping it around. I saw evidence of mouse droppings in the shed. You're going to need a cat if you don't want the mice coming inside the house."

A shiver of revulsion slithered up her spine. She'd been chased by Fredrik holding a live mouse more than once. She'd been scared of them ever since. Defeat left a bitter taste in her mouth, but he was right. The cat would stay and earn its keep. "It can stay, but I'm not keeping the kittens."

The cat yawned.

Fredrik looked miffed, his brow lifting. "*Ya,* sure." He didn't sound confident at all, but he wasn't backing down. "Ulla and John are always in need of a good barn cat. I'll find them all homes."

"Do you have any grand ideas where we should put her for the night?" She looked up and found Fredrik watching her.

"What?" she asked. Why was he looking at her like that?

He smiled at her. Really smiled. Not just the grin of a friendly man, but a man who might see her as acceptable. A smile that reached all the way up to his eyes.

She grew flustered, her face warming. She had work to do. He could take that cat out to the shed, make it a bed and go.

She knew how to get rid of him. "Rumor has it you're looking for a wife. That so?"

"*Ya,*" he muttered, his expression becoming serious. "Why do you ask?" He went back to stroking the cat, his intense, blue-eyed gaze remaining on her.

"No reason. I was just wondering, is all."

"You planning on applying for the job?"

"Me? *Nee.* I'm a new widow with a child to raise and now kittens to look after, thanks to you."

Fredrik straightened himself and headed for the door, his boots making noise against the hardwood floors as he shuffled past her. "I think kitty and I will be out in the shed if you need us."

Lizbeth picked up a box of crumpled newspapers left over from the unpacked dishes. "You can take this with you, if you don't mind," she said.

He grabbed the edge of the box. "You're different now, you know." His gaze wandered over her face.

"You're still the same. A jokester, always pulling pranks at everyone else's expense."

Fredrik stepped into the hall, but looked back. "I'm sure I am, but it makes me wonder what made you so bitter and out of sorts."

She wiped her hand down her apron, her remorse lowering her head. "It's just been a long day...a long week."

"*Ya*, it has. Perhaps a day at the fair would put you in a better mood," he said with a smile that made her legs grow weak. "I'm going tomorrow after work. Would you and Benuel like to come with me?"

"*Nee*, but *danki*, Fredrik. I already promised Ulla I'd go with her and the sewing ladies."

"Perhaps another time. There's always the Christmas auction," he suggested, patting his hat in place.

Her heart skipped a beat. "*Ya*, that sounds *gut*."

"*Ya*, it does. Well, good night," he said with a fresh smile and turned to go.

"Good night," she murmured, listening to the sound of his footfalls as he ambled through the house and out the front door.

She hung her head. *Gott* had to be disappointed in her. Just because she was bone tired didn't mean she could behave in such a way with Fredrik. He was only trying to be a help to her. She shuffled back toward the kitchen. It seemed the man wanted nothing more than to be her friend. He had no real interest in her as a prospective bride. Which was exactly what she wanted. So why was it so disappointing?

Chapter Eight

～❧～

"Who'll give me sixteen fifty?" the auction-eer called out.

Several hands flew up. The crowd of auction-goers formed a tight knot, their placards waving, hoping to be seen.

He waited, his left hand shading his eyes from the bright Florida sun overhead. "Do I hear seventeen fifty, now eighteen?" A warm summer afternoon sweat dampened the man's shirt a darker blue around his neck and ringed his armpits.

He squinted, scanning the swarm of Amish, Mennonite and *Englischers* milling around the front of his improvised auction stand. He appeared content to wait a few moments longer to see if the price would advance.

Fredrik lifted his number high. "Twenty-five dollars," he shouted over the hum of the generator vibrating behind him. The shelf would fit perfectly over the toilet in the apartment and add much-needed storage to the tiny bathroom space he was remodeling. He hoped to find some spare time to work on the place, if work at the furniture store slowed down.

The auctioneer's long gray beard touched the front of his pale blue shirt as he nodded his silver head in approval and pointed in Fredrik's direction. "Fair warning...and it's gone, gone, gone at twenty-five dollars and not a penny more."

Motioned forward, Fredrik wove his way toward the front of the crowd. An Amish teenager of fifteen or sixteen, with a bad complexion and a full head of dark hair, handed over the shelf. "Pay my *mamm* over there," the boy muttered and pointed to a tiny woman sitting at a table under a moss-covered shade tree.

"*Ya*, sure," Fredrik agreed and strode away, only to step into the path of a running child.

To keep from knocking the boy down, he had to grab hold of the child's black suspenders. He was surprised to see he had young Benuel Mullet, Lizbeth's son, in tow.

"What are you doing running around all by yourself?" he asked. The boy's sweaty face scrunched up, his bottom lip quivering as he prepared to cry. Fredrik skimmed the faces around them. Lizbeth had to be somewhere close by. "Where's your *mamm*?"

"Let me be," Benuel wailed in *Deitch* as he twisted and kicked at Fredrik's shin.

"Not till you tell me where your *mamm* is, young man. I have a feeling she hasn't a clue where you are."

"*Ya*, she does," he declared. A tear glistened in his eye as he pointed to a fenced-in children's pool filled with water and crowded with fluffy yellow ducklings. "She promised I could see the baby ducks my *grossdaddi* is selling."

The boy nervously glanced over his shoulder and peered into the crowd of shoppers behind them. Lizbeth, wearing a dress of pale blue cotton, surged from a group of local women in their customary *kapps* and aprons and rushed forward. Her long legs ate up the distance between them. Normally pale cheeked, her face glowed from her exertion in the hot afternoon sun. A vexed expression creased her forehead into deep lines, indicating to Fredrik that she might have been searching for the boy awhile.

"Thank you for catching him," she said.

He released Benuel's narrow suspenders and stepped back.

Benuel's small body stilled. He wiped away the dampness from his eyes and watched his mother advance. "*Grossdaddi* said I could see the ducks," he called to her.

Lizbeth scooped up the small boy. "You scared the life from me. Do you know that?" She kissed the boy's cheeks and then his hair and pulled him close. "I thought you'd been taken." She sent a look of appreciation Fredrik's way.

Benuel wiggled in her arms. "I just wanted—"

"*Ya*, I know. You want to see those silly ducks swim." She hugged him close, even though he pushed at her with his small hands. "Didn't your *grossdaddi* promise to take you later, after we ate? Always stay with me, Benuel. Never wander off alone." She looked into his eyes. "We're not on the farm now. There are hidden dangers in Pinecraft from cars on the streets and crowds of strangers."

The boy's eyes widened.

Fredrik took in a deep breath. The boy needed the firm hand of a father, not the scary tales about danger his mother was telling him. He had been a boy much like Benuel. Always running off, giving his mother reason to worry. Lizbeth needed help raising the boy. That much was certain-sure.

Preoccupied with thoughts of Benuel, Fredrik waved goodbye to Lizbeth and strolled away, merging into the crowd around him. He stood under the shade of an ancient oak tree watching mother and son from a distance. Was he the man to help raise the boy? Lizbeth was a fine woman. A devoted *mamm*. He'd be proud to call her his *fraa*. He longed to help teach the boy how to behave and grow into a *gut* man. Something unexplainable drew him to Lizbeth and her son.

In frustration, he kicked at a stone on the path and sent it flying into the gnarled trunk of a palm tree at the edge of the largest auction tent. Was Lizbeth the woman for him? She was available, but a grieving widow. Perhaps he should step back awhile and wait on *Gott*'s direction.

He cast her a veiled glance and headed back under the large tent where another auction was about to start. He contemplated his odd behavior of late. When had Lizbeth Mullet gotten so deeply under his skin? Was he falling in love with the widow?

By late afternoon the auctions under the big tent were in full swing. Lizbeth watched people mill around, their chatter sounding like the constant hum of a bee's nest. The blue tarp, stretched taut by ropes, provided shade for the local sewing ladies all dressed in varying shades of pale lavender, blue and yellow. The covering danced and flapped overhead as a gust of wind swirled across the park and deposited dead leaves at their feet.

Lizbeth plunged her short quilting needle into the soft layers of cotton for safekeeping and then stomped her old black lace-up shoes, sending leaves flying. She went back to making tiny stitches on the beautiful double-wedding-ring quilt the sewing group was finishing for Bertha Zook's December wedding.

Thankfully she hadn't forgotten everything she knew about quilting while she'd been in Ohio. Her mother-in-law had never allowed her to sit in with the local sewing group. She was seldom allowed to go into town for groceries or fabric for clothes, and when she did, Jonah was always with her. The ladies of the community came routinely to the farm to sew, but Lizbeth was always banished to her bedroom, as if she were an embarrassment to the family. It had been another way to humiliate her, which seemed to bring pleasure to the mean-spirited older woman.

"You ready to move in to your new home, Lizbeth?" Kitty Troyer asked, her brown-eyed gaze darting toward Lizbeth and then back to the row of minute stitches she was making on her end of the quilt. As habit would have it, a tiny wedge of her pink tongue stuck out as she concentrated on what she was doing with her needle.

"Benuel and I should finish moving in soon," Lizbeth answered. But was she ready to move in to the big house with a *kinner* and live alone for the first time in her life? Most of her belongings, meager as they were, already hung in the generous closets, sat on the newly papered shelves. Benuel's shirts and britches were folded in the old, but well-preserved, dresser in the smaller room next to hers.

She'd managed to delay the actual move-in date, but she'd run out of time. Most of the house repairs had been made by Fredrik and her *daed*, with the exception of a short list, including new tile floors that were to be laid some time next week.

It was move in or admit she wasn't ready to be a single parent to Benuel. Did she have the parenting skills needed to keep such an overactive child contained? She doubted she did, but she was learning fast and would soon have them. The night before it had taken the joined efforts of her *daed*, Ulla and herself to get Benuel to bed. He'd been placed back in his cot over and over, threatened with punishment by her father, but still he'd resisted. Later, he had snuck into her bed late in the night, while everyone was asleep.

Beyond exhausted, she'd allowed him to sleep with her for a few additional minutes and then carried him back to his bed, only to find him snuggled under her quilt when the sunshine came streaming into her bedroom window this morning.

She couldn't keep allowing him to sleep in her bed. He was getting too big. He needed to catch up with other boys his age.

She'd struggled to teach him to tie his own shoes before breakfast, promising him the treat of his favorite pancakes if he'd just listen to her instructions and try for himself. His mind didn't seem able to settle on what she'd been telling him. For mere seconds he'd paid attention and then was off to watch a ladybug crawl on the screen door. She'd ended up tying his shoes for him and sending him off to brush his teeth.

The doctor she'd taken him to just after Jonah's death had diagnosed him with ADHD. She'd been given a pamphlet. The doctor's comments clarified why Benuel had such a hard time learning new skills and why he was never able to sit still long enough to listen to words of instruction. But knowing the name of the problem didn't make him any easier to teach.

The doctor had spoken of medication that

could be used when he was older and in school. The pamphlets she'd read and placed on the table had turned up missing, no doubt thrown out by her father-in-law, who swore there was nothing wrong with the boy that a good whipping wouldn't cure. It was that man's answer for everything.

Lost in her own world, Lizbeth didn't hear her name being called until Ulla touched her arm.

Lizbeth glanced up, acknowledging Ulla with a glance and then noticed all the women around the quilting hoop looking her way. She'd known some of the older women most of her life. A few were strangers to her, but they all accepted her in a way that told her she was welcomed to the sewing circle. She scrambled to remember what the topic of conversation had been a moment before. She felt her face warm. "I'm sorry. Was someone speaking to me?"

At the far end of the large square hoop, Theda Fischer, the bishop's wife, leaned forward and spoke, a tiny dimple appearing as she smiled sweetly Lizbeth's way. The day's humidity had the older woman's crisp *kapp* floating atop a mass of frazzled reddish-gray hair. "*Ya*, it was me, Lizzy. I was wondering if you'd be starting Benuel at the Mennonite school. There'll be two openings now that Henry Schrock took his twins back to live with his *mamm*."

Benuel's birthday was in a few days. He'd turn five and be old enough to attend. But she hadn't considered putting him in school since his behavior had become so volatile of late. She'd decided to wait a bit, at least until he turned six.

If he *were* an average boy of five, she thought, she'd consider sending him. But sadly, he wasn't. He was a handful, even for her *daed*, who had managed to keep her rambunctious brother in line until he'd been baptized and married at twenty-four. "He seems so young to be cooped up in a classroom all those hours. Perhaps it's best…" Lizbeth let her words float away on the breeze, not sure what else to add.

After threading another needle, Theda glanced back at her. "Mark my words. It's the best thing that could happen to a young man with his level of intelligence and energy."

So others in the small community *had* noticed Benuel's inability to contain himself. Lizbeth thrust her needle in the fabric and pricked herself. Careful not to get the droplet of blood on the quilt, she jerked her handkerchief from her apron and wrapped it around her finger. "Time will tell," she offered and went back to sewing.

Around the hoop several ladies murmured their opinions. Lizbeth glanced over at Ulla and watched as her father's new wife smoothed the quilt out in front of her and tightened her edge of the hoop. She affectionately shared a smile with Lizbeth.

A moment later Lizbeth glanced back up as Ulla murmured to no one in particular, "It makes me to wonder if all this talk of Benuel's behavior and the merits of school isn't stressing Lizbeth. We must remember she *is* a new widow, with enough on her plate for now. She's dealing with the loss of her beloved husband, and moving in to a new home. Instead of us concerning ourselves with the pros and cons of school, let's sing some songs and lighten her spirits."

A nervous giggle came from Pearly, the community's favorite soloist at their local New Order Amish church. Ulla nodded her way and the sweet words of "I'll Meet You in The Morning" began in the woman's high, clear voice, leaving Lizbeth time to gather her troubled thoughts.

As she sang along, she contemplated her and Benuel's future. The choices she'd make in the next few weeks could change the little boy's life. She wanted what was best for him, wanted him to grow into a fine, strong man, with or without a father around to guide him. Benuel would have her *daed* as a guiding light and he would have to be enough. He was a far cry better than Benuel's last stand-in father.

Sunlight filtering through the trees revealed Fredrik walking past their little canvas-topped island. He was with a man Lizbeth recognized as Lon Yoder, one of their classmates back in school. He and Fredrik pulled at the rims of their straw hats and nodded in her direction as they silently passed.

She was careful to take in a slow breath and not let anyone see how thrilled she really was to be near Fredrik again. She'd had a crush on him as a girl, and she'd thought it could turn into more. But then he'd walked out of her life without so much as a wave goodbye. Someday he might make a good husband, but not yet. Besides, she wasn't sure she'd ever be ready to marry. Would she be able to trust a man again? To love again? She hoped so.

A cooling breeze ruffled her hair and brought her back to her surroundings. She looped a strand of hair behind her ear and picked up her needle. Fredrik was out of sight, lost in the sea of people mingling around. She tried to quiet her thoughts, but her heart kept beating loudly in her ears.

She glanced around the quilting hoop. The

singing had ended and several of the ladies where chatting amongst themselves, sharing stories about new grandbabies or the friendly *Englischer* who'd taken their pictures when they'd met on the street and then offered them a dollar in payment. Lizbeth resumed her work on the quilt, determined in her heart to do her best for Benuel as he grew into a man of faith.

Chapter Nine

The wind caught the farmhouse door and slammed it shut with a bang behind Lizbeth's father and Fredrik Lapp.

Seeing them walk in, Lizbeth lowered her eyes and steadied her hand as she placed a steaming bowl of homegrown string beans on the table. "Is Fredrik eating with us tonight?" Her heart skipped a beat, reminding her of her growing attraction to the man. She smoothed out wrinkles from the simple white tablecloth covering the table before heading back toward the kitchen for the pot roast, new potatoes and carrots platter.

Ulla's eyes darted toward the front of the house. A corner of her mouth lifted. "*Ya.* He's ready to start work on the apartment behind the house and needs John's advice on some of the projects. Your *daed* told me he'd invited

Fredrik to stay for dinner a while ago. I just forgot to tell you."

Lizbeth's brows lifted. She tried hard not to smile and show the joy she felt. She was acting like a silly teen and knew it. "That's fine with me."

Ulla slipped Lizbeth a curious glance and then went back to stirring tiny lumps out of John's favorite brown gravy bubbling in the iron skillet. "You don't have any feelings for Fredrik, do you?"

Lizbeth brushed away a ringlet of hair from her forehead and then reached overhead for the gravy boat her mother had always used for special occasions such as this. It was Benuel's fifth birthday, a reason to celebrate. "*Nee*. Not a bit."

She felt her face warm because of her lie. She'd have to repent during bedtime prayers. "I was just wondering, is all," she added and placed the bowl in front of Ulla, watching as the thick mixture of browned flour, chicken broth, thick cream, and salt and pepper was poured into the fragile, spouted container. When it was full to overflowing, Lizbeth wiped the sides of the old dish and carried it over to the condiments tray. She waited for Ulla to lead the way back to the table being readied for their meal.

Ulla carried in a covered basket of piping hot rolls and positioned them next to the steaming meat platter. Her face was flushed from working over a hot stove. She favored the right knee she'd injured stepping on one of Benuel's small cars left on the floor. The hobbling woman whispered over her shoulder, "The man's always seemed nice to me. Maybe you should show him some interest. I hear he's looking for a *fraa*." She smiled and looked hopeful. "He'd make a *gut* father for Benuel."

Lizbeth faked a smile. The last thing she needed was to fall for Fredrik Lapp again, or let Benuel get too attached to him, and have him chose another woman for his *fraa*.

John strode into the dining room with Fredrik trailing close behind. Her father grinned over at Ulla and then dipped his head in a friendly manner at Lizbeth as he removed his sweaty hat. His gray hair was trimmed shorter than usual, exposing the generous ears *Gott* had blessed him with. He hitched up his overlong trouser legs by pulling on his drooping black suspenders and headed for his usual chair at the big wooden table.

"I see Ulla finally caught you unawares with scissors in hand," Lizbeth teased, causing her father to laugh in a robust manner.

"She did, indeed," he admitted and impatiently beckoned for the younger man to sit next to him. "Sit there, Fredrik. Next to Lizbeth and me."

Hat in hand, Fredrik pulled out a chair and lowered himself, his gaze shifting to Lizbeth, who stood across the table from him.

She smiled his way and felt her stomach tighten.

He smiled back, his eyes sparkling.

She tried not to show how thrilled she was. Her affection toward the man was getting out of hand. She'd have to control her emotions.

"I'm sure you ladies have prepared enough food," Fredrik said. He licked his lips, flashed a nervous smile.

Ulla threw her head back and chuckled. "Have you ever known me to cook small meals, Fredrik? Every night I cook enough food for five hearty men." She grabbed the back of the chair closest to John, pulled it out and lowered herself with a groan.

"I'll…ah…just go get Benuel and *daed*'s hound," Lizbeth stammered. "He and that dog should be tired of feeding those chickens by now." She found her hand nervously patting her loose bun, her fingers toying with the hairs curling around her neck as she marched to the back door. Did she look a mess? It seemed the man always caught her in her worst moments.

As soon as she realized what she was doing

she mentally scolded herself, her face flaming as she stepped onto the back porch. What foolishness. So what if her hair was flying around her face in a haphazard way. She secured her wayward curls with pins and shoved her *kapp* down on the back of her head.

"Supper time. Come get your hands washed," she called out. She saw the boy and dog rush to the barn to put away the bag of cracked corn he was dragging along the ground behind him.

"*Ya*, I'm coming," he called out with a wave.

This was Benuel's special day. It wasn't every day a boy turned five. "Quick. Come," she said in old *Deitch* and beckoned him up the steps.

Fredrik cut into the tender pot roast and stifled a groan of delight as he chewed the delicious morsel. John and Ulla had always made him feel welcome at their table, but it was Lizbeth's smile that warmed him—and made him a bit uncomfortable.

Benuel's short legs kicked back and forth as he played with his food, less than a mouthful eaten the whole time he'd been sitting in his chair. "Can I have cake now?" he asked, his words directed to his mother across from him.

"Once you finish your food," she said and speared a wedge of carrot off her plate.

"But I don't like—"

Fredrik interrupted, "When I was your age I ate all my vegetables and my *bruder*'s, too. My *mamm* said they built big muscles." He flexed his arm and showed off a well-rounded biceps to the boy. "See."

Benuel's eyes grew round with wonder. "Is so?" he asked his *mamm*, his look skeptical.

"*Ya*, is so." She bobbed her head. She had seemed impressed with the flex of his muscles, too.

Hesitant, Benuel broke off the tiniest sliver of potato and thrust it in his mouth. "I don't like how they taste," he said, and laid down his fork.

"Never mind," Fredrik muttered and shoveled in a mound of potatoes slathered in melted butter. "I'll eat your share. I need to keep up my strength for the shuffleboard game tomorrow."

"I've never played shuffleboard," Benuel informed him. "My *mamm* says I'm too little."

Fredrik smacked the bottom of the ketchup bottle and drowned his perfectly cooked beef in a sea of red sauce. "It makes me to wonder if you're too little because you leave your vegetables on your plate and not in your stomach."

Benuel pressed his lips together and kicked at the chair leg under him. "*Ya*, well. I don't want to play shuffleboard anyway. The game looks dumb." He impatiently brushed away a curl falling down on his forehead, his gaze on the offending vegetables.

"Don't kick your chair at the table," Lizbeth reminded the boy as she laid down her fork and knife next to her plate. She cocked her head and smiled. "Why don't you eat the last of your dinner? I'm sure everyone's wanting to have some chocolate birthday cake." Her tone was light and affectionate.

Ulla smiled her encouragement to Benuel and took a bite of her own vegetables.

John ate the last bite of the thick slab of beef that had been on his plate and rubbed his protruding stomach in satisfaction. "Some say that sauce makes anything green taste better." He gestured toward the ketchup bottle and relocated it close to Benuel.

The young boy looked at his grandfather and nibbled on his bottom lip, contemplating the advice while he looked at the bottle.

John shoved his empty plate forward. "It matters not to me whether you get cake. I'm having mine with ice cream and sprinkles."

Benuel gave a shrug of defeat and grabbed the bottle of sauce. Three insignificant drops fell on the single slice of carrot on his plate. He shoved his hair away from his face again and then drove his fork into the glazed wedge.

Fredrik found himself holding his breath. Silence filled the room, all eyes on the child who had disrupted the entire meal with his complaints.

The boy gingerly put the bite in his mouth and chewed. He lifted his chin and eyed his grandfather with new respect. "*Ya*, it is *gut*," he said and covered his potatoes in a circle of red.

Fredrik watched as the tension drained from Lizbeth's face. She brightened, her eyes sparkling from the overhead light.

"I'll go get the cake now." She slid a guarded look at Benuel and then hurried away.

Fredrik cleared his throat, surprised at the level of emotion he felt for the young boy. It had to be hard losing his father and moving to a new place, seeing all new faces around him. "John, why don't you come to the shuffleboard game with us tomorrow? I hear there's going to be a competition between the boys and the men. You could bring Benuel with you." He put his hands on the table and turned to Benuel. "You're sure to win eating all those vegetables," he told the boy with a grin.

"*Ya*, that sounds *gut*," John said and they both looked toward the doorway.

Lizbeth stood in the door's arch, listening to their chatter, the simple cake in her hands. A silly grin played on her lips.

* * *

Lizbeth sat the cake on the middle of the table. "Who wants a slice?" she asked. Her breath was ragged from rushing, but she rose to the occasion and began to sing the birthday song to her son in their native tongue. She cut thick wedges for everyone but herself.

Benuel received his cake first and then her father, who nodded his approval. Ulla was next. When she handed Fredrik his plate, she made sure her fingers were well away from his reach, and then cut the thinnest sliver for herself and sat. She watched as Benuel dug into the rich chocolate cake and poked a huge bite into his mouth. He smiled her way, his top lip circled in the thick chocolate icing she'd made this morning.

"It's certain-sure *gut*," he said, licking his lips with his tongue.

Lizbeth continued to watch the child, the love she felt for him brightening her mood. He was growing up too fast. He would be her only child. She was determined to enjoy his younger years while she could.

A fleeting moment of remorse cut through her. If by some twist of fate, she and Fredrik did marry, would she be able to give him a half-dozen sons? The doctor had never said for sure she could carry another *boppli* to term.

She frowned, her disappointment weighing her down. She couldn't continue to encourage the man. He deserved more children than just Benuel. She thrust away her regrets and enjoyed the smile on Benuel's face. Today she'd concentrate on him. Tomorrow she'd figure out a way to keep Fredrik out of her life, even if the thought broke her heart.

Chapter Ten

Fredrik skidded to a stop and fell to the ground, his legs imprisoned by a laughing Mennonite boy of ten or twelve. Minor pain in his left elbow told him he wasn't completely over the fall he'd taken when he'd almost run over Lizbeth and Benuel.

He kept his smile pasted to his face, but the memory of almost killing them was still too fresh in his mind. He snatched his straw hat off the ground and pushed his hair out of his eyes before placing it back on his head. He knew *Gott* had forgiven him, but he hung on to his remorse as a humbling lesson. One day he'd forgive himself, but not today.

Mennonite and Amish men and their sons wandered across the field and started another free-for-all football game. He wished young Benuel had been allowed to come to the park with his grandfather. The boy would have enjoyed the opportunity to run wild and not be watched so closely by his *mamm*. The child was hyperactive, prone to getting into mischief, just as he'd been as a boy. He understood the need for speed and the urge to talk too much.

Fredrik accepted the hand that reached out to help him up and scrambled to his feet. A chuckle escaped him. He, and everyone around him, found his clumsiness amusing. Head down, he dusted the dirt off his shirtsleeve, and then congratulated the boy who'd brought him down. "You've got great tackling skills," he said, with a firm pat on the back. "*Gut* job." He watched the boy run across the field to join his friends. "I think I'm getting too old for this game," he remarked.

"*Ya*, could be," Mose Fischer commented from behind him and laughed when Fredrik turned and made a face.

"I noticed you took a few spills yourself this afternoon, elder Fischer," Fredrik shot back and snickered at his boss's counterfeit wounded expression.

"That I did," Mose admitted and pointed to a tear in his pants. "Sarah will be grievously offended by my abuse to the new trousers she stitched this week."

Someone snatched up the football and kicked

it high in the air. The game was on again, but Fredrik and Mose lagged behind, letting the younger boys keep the games going. "I'm ready for some cold lemonade."

"*Ya*, me too." Fredrik nodded, and then paused just long enough to brush grass off his green-stained trouser leg. "Are Sarah and the *kinner* with you today?"

"*Nee*. She and Ulla took the *kinner* to see how Lizbeth is faring at the house. I hear she's got her hands full with that young boy of hers. Beatrice tells me he's a real stinker."

Fredrik's mouth twitched in a lopsided grin. "That he is."

Mose glanced his way. "Lizbeth's about your age. Were you scholars together?"

"We were. I used to run around with her *bruder* as a boy and her *mamm* would send Lizbeth along for good measure." He chortled. "She used to drive us crazy." He tugged at his straw hat, his memories of a younger, skinnier version of Lizbeth causing him to smile broadly. "She talked too much and was always into mischief."

"Like Benuel?" Mose asked, wiping sweat from his glistening forehead.

"*Nee*, not like him. Lizbeth got into innocent mischief, but Benuel's behavior is different." He laughed at his own ridiculous thought. "He's more like I was as a boy. Easily distracted. Always into trouble or getting paddled for doing something stupid."

"If he's hyper like you, then I'd say poor kid and poor Lizbeth." Mose laughed. "I was older than you, but I remember you tearing around the playground full tilt, knocking down girls and making them cry."

Fredrik dropped his head and faked remorse. "*Ya*. My *mamm* used to say she held her breath until I went to bed each night."

"Beatrice took a liking to Benuel right off," Mose said, "but then swore he hit her. She's not so enamored with the boy now."

They both laughed at the thought of Mose's outspoken eldest daughter, Beatrice, and Benuel in the same room together. "I'm sure she'll change her mind about him when they get a bit older," Fredrik said, and couldn't resist adding, "One day you might find her married to Chicken John's grandson."

Mose stopped, squeezed his eyes shut for a second and then looked up into the sky. "Don't wish that on me. Can you imagine what my grandchildren would be like?"

Fredrik thought about an older Mose holding grandchildren in his arms. He could see it, but couldn't see himself with children yet, much less grandchildren. If he didn't start stepping out soon he wouldn't have a wife to share grandchildren with. Lizbeth's face came to his mind, her butter-blond hair blowing around it. The widow interested him deeply, but was she ready for marriage? Would she consider him good husband material? She knew him too well, so probably not.

The next day Lizbeth couldn't believe her eyes. Hands high on her hips, she bellowed, "Benuel James Mullet! Put down that nasty frog and come into the house right now. Wash your hands. Do you want to get warts?"

She gasped as she watched Benuel kiss the slimy frog on the head again. With all the tenderness of a mother, he placed the speckled critter back on the ground and encouraged it along with the wave of his small hands.

"I'll come find you later and we'll play," he said loud enough for his mother to hear. He shot her an accusing glance as the frog seemed to understand his words and worked its way under the root of an old moss-covered tree.

"You will not find him later. You'll leave that nasty frog alone and any other wild critters you find in this backyard." She wiped her hands on her clean work apron as if she felt the slime on them, and laughed. She knew what frogs felt like thanks to her brother's and Fredrik Lapp's practical jokes back in school. At least once a week she would find one in her lunch bag or stuck down in one of her shoes. She fought the urge to cringe. She knew boys loved their lizards and toads, but she was determined not to find one in her *soh*'s trouser pockets come wash day.

Benuel stomped past her, his lips pouted. "He was my only friend and now he's gone." His head dropped as he rounded the corner of the house and made a hasty retreat for the kitchen door.

Maybe she'd been too harsh on the child. She was repulsed by frogs, but he wasn't. She had to let him be himself. Like what he liked. He was growing up, would want to discover the wonders of the world for himself.

A glance at his retreating back told her his clothes were getting too small, the hems of his trousers exposing his bony ankles. She'd have to get out her *mamm*'s old sewing machine and stitch up two pairs of trousers and a new shirt for church. Sewing men's clothes had never been one of her strong suits, but Sarah Fischer had offered to give her a refresher class with a few other women from the community.

The back door banged shut. She hurried along. There was lunch to prepare, laundry to wash and she needed to buy a bag of food for the cat out in the shed. This morning she'd found evidence the cat's midnight hunts were paying off. The little mother-to-be was earning her keep. She'd had to throw a long, skinny rat tail away before Benuel found it and kept it as a souvenir.

Lizbeth heard the water splashing in the front bathroom. A moment later, Benuel came into the kitchen, his hands dripping water all over her freshly mopped kitchen floor. "Did you dry your hands?"

He looked down at his still-moist hands and nodded. "I think so."

She tossed him a kitchen towel and suggested, "Perhaps not as well as you could have."

His casual shrug told her how worried he was to have damp hands. He pulled out a chair and plopped himself down, his legs still going at a fast clip. Back and forth. Back and forth.

Lizbeth took in a deep breath and turned back to the beef patties she was forming. How did it feel, this ADHD? It couldn't be easy dealing with the constant urge to be in motion, your mind racing before you could complete a thought. "Would you like cheese on your burger?"

"No. Just ketchup," he said, his fingers tapping out a tune only he heard.

Two extra bottles of red sauce waited in the

kitchen closet. Since her father had suggested vegetables tasted better with sauce on them, the boy ate everything with a good dousing. There was no way hot oatmeal could taste better with butter, maple syrup and ketchup, but Benuel had gobbled it down this morning. She wasn't going to complain. No fussing over food was fine with her.

"Why is that man in our back garden?"

Lizbeth pulled back the curtain and peered out the kitchen window. "What man?"

He wrote his name in the salt he'd sprinkled on the table.

"Don't waste the salt and make a mess." She watched a dark form become the shape of a man and realized it was Fredrik working on the back apartment. Banging began. "That's Fredrik, our landlord. How long has he been out there?" The sun was shining, and it was warm out, but Fredrik had no hat covering his ginger hair.

"I don't know. He was there when I went out."

The hammering stopped. Fredrik moved out of sight. Lizbeth, who was tall for a woman, stretched to see where he had gone. Her sight was encumbered by a row of leafy trees lining the back fence. "Was he friendly?"

"*Ya*. He said he likes kids and frogs."

Sizzling fat popped out of the frying pan and hit her on the arm. She flipped over the burgers and put a bun on the gas burner to toast. "You're not to bother him while he works, do you hear?"

"I'm hungry. Is the meat cooked yet?" he said, ignoring her comment. With a flourish, he added pepper to the mess he was making on the tablecloth and squiggled his name in it. He sneezed twice and then used his hand to remove the mess he'd made.

"I asked you a question. Did you bother him while he was working?" She turned the gas off under the toasted bun and used a fork to place it on the plate, and then added the burger before she turned around.

Benuel ran his hands through his hair, dislodging a leaf and tree bark and placing them where the salt and pepper had been. "I don't remember." His expression looked sincere.

Lizbeth sat the boy's food in front of him and placed the ketchup next to his plate. "Was he working hard?"

He grinned and grabbed the red bottle in front of him. "*Ya*. He's nailing in new wood around the door." He dumped a circle of red on his plate. "Stuff like that."

The banging began again. She glanced toward the window, watched the breeze flip the curtain in a swirl. Fredrik's back came into view, his blue shirtsleeve stretching taut as he lifted his arm and swung the hammer in his hand. It seemed he was everywhere she went, or was she just noticing him because she liked being around him? This foolish attraction to the man had to stop. He needed a wife to give him children and there was no guarantee she could do that, even if she was interested in finding a new husband.

"*Nee!* Don't do that," she scolded as she turned back toward her son, but it was too late. Benuel had already dunked his burger in a pool of ketchup. He smiled in satisfaction as he chewed, and took another big bite of hamburger slathered in red sauce. He ignored her comment.

Lizbeth shrugged her shoulders and went back to washing dishes. At least he was eating now. Maybe she'd try some lettuce and tomato on his bun the next time. Eating this hardy, he just might put some weight on at last, and she had Fredrik and her father to thank for it.

Fredrik had already fixed the broken gutter over the apartment door, but the damage had allowed wood rot to form at the base of the door. He yanked on the crumbling wood with a crowbar, cleaned out the leaves and dirt and then replaced the length of wood with a fresh board. Content, he hummed as he nailed the wood into place. He'd paint the strip later, while he sanded and painted the peeling front door. The small concrete porch was intact and the sidewalk to the wire gate seemed fit enough, even though there was a slight crack in one section.

Lizbeth's kitchen window was open. Perhaps her cooking was the source of the delicious aroma floating on the late-afternoon breeze. His stomach grumbled. It had been a long time since lunch.

Two days a week he worked half days at Mose's furniture barn. Being off today gave him the opportunity to do a few jobs on the apartment and some of the handyman jobs he had lined up around Pinecraft and Sarasota, but they sure messed with his eating schedule.

He checked his pocket watch and snapped it shut, surprised to see it was already six, an hour past his usual dinner meal. He would stop soon and grab a bite to eat at the café, but he still had a lot of work to do. He wanted to rent the apartment before the month ended since he had decided to sublet it for profit.

Sweat beaded his forehead. He swiped at it, and then banged another nail into the wood.

He slipped the hammer into his waist belt, heard the sound of a child giggling and turned to see Benuel running out the side door of the white house.

"Come back and let me wipe your face," Lizbeth shouted, hot on her son's heels. The gate slammed behind the boy. His mother managed to seize his arm before he could climb into the swing hanging from the old oak tree covered in moss.

Memories of his childhood and his *mamm* having to haul him back into the house for a good face scrubbing flashed in his mind. *Boys will be boys*, his *daed* used to tell her when she complained about his lack of table manners at the supper table.

Boys needed a man in their lives, someone to show them how to behave and still have fun. He was glad to be around to see Benuel at his best, when he was relaxed and growing more secure in his new home.

Too hungry to wait to eat, he packed up his tools, locked the apartment door and then glanced back to Lizbeth. He watched as she scrubbed at Benuel's face with a cloth. The boy squirmed and kicked just like Fredrik used to fight his *mamm* at that age. Lizbeth looked like she'd been busy, her hair wild under her *kapp* in the fading light of day. Her cheeks were rosy from the heat of the kitchen. Smudges of something she'd been cooking were wiped down the front of her apron, making her look adorable. He wanted a wife like her. Someone who took care of her family and loved them.

He couldn't help but laugh when Benuel got away. The memory of the thrill of the chase was still so alive in Fredrik's mind that he took in a deep breath of excitement. He let loose a guffaw as mother and son ran around the yard, her skirts swirling, the boy's long legs making fast work of the distance between him and the swing.

Benuel pumped himself high into the air. Lizbeth stood a yard away, her hands dangling at her sides. Frustration etched lines across her forehead. "You have to come off that swing sometime, young man. And when you do, your face is mine."

"A little dirt won't hurt him," Fredrik supposed out loud.

Lizbeth turned just her head in his direction. She smiled her welcome. "No. A bit of dirt won't hurt him, but him not listening to me might. I'm trying to teach him to obey."

Fredrik did his best to sober his expression, but knew he'd failed miserably. He nodded his head. "*Ya*, you're certain-sure right. *Mamms* always are." He glanced back at Benuel. The child was ignoring them both, the wind blowing his ginger hair into spikes, his boyish voice singing a simple children's worship song Fredrik had sung himself at the boy's age.

A smile lifted one side of Lizbeth's mouth as she listened to Benuel sing.

"He has a good, strong voice," Fredrik commented, but continued to walk toward his bike resting at the side of the shed.

"*Ya*, he does. Like my *daed*," she muttered, more to herself than to him.

He walked his bike to the gate, considering the lonely mood that had come over him. He was tired of being alone. He would have rather gone into Lizbeth's kitchen and settled himself in one of her chairs than go to the café and eat alone. Sharing a meal with her and the boy would have been a treat.

When had he begun to think this way... begun to seriously long for a family of his own? This family? "Have a good night," he called, waving as he threw his leg over the bike.

She turned and waved back, her expression friendly and relaxed. "And you, Fredrik Lapp."

He headed north and minutes later turned into the graveled parking lot across from the café. He'd have to seriously begin his search for a wife. It was past time to settle, begin a family of his own, but first he'd have to see if Lizbeth would have him. He just had to find the nerve to ask her. If she wasn't interested, he needed to pull back and put some distance between them. Fredrik wasn't willing to risk his heart once more.

Benuel's voice still sounded in his subconscious, putting a smile on Fredrik's face. He lifted his head, looked at the darkening sky. What a shame Lizbeth seemed so uneasy about sharing her life again.

From the way she distanced herself from all men, perhaps he knew he didn't have a chance with her now, but he wouldn't give up easily. She was a fine woman, a woman who needed a father for her son. He thought of the soft curve of her cheek, the way her eyes sparkled when she was happy. Perhaps he *was* the man meant to put a smile back on her face and she just didn't realize it yet.

He walked into the café humming the childish song Benuel had been singing about letting his light shine for Jesus. Would Fredrik continue to hide his light under a bucket? *Nee*, he didn't think so.

Chapter Eleven

The first two weeks in the rental house had gone smoother than Lizbeth had expected. Fredrik was often underfoot with this project or that, but she'd grown comfortable with his sudden appearances. When he used Benuel as his helper, it freed her up to cook special meals they could share together. Was it so wrong to feel as if they were becoming a family of sorts?

She tossed in her bed. The nights were hard on her. She heard every groan and moan the old house made, knew when Benuel turned in his small bed.

Unable to sleep, she'd let the young mama cat in for company and found herself petting her as she prepared to put another load of colored clothes in the washing machine. She was grateful Fredrik had left it for his renters to use.

As they walked into the kitchen, the cat indicated she'd like to go out. Lizbeth opened the side door a crack and watched the cat's belly sway from side to side as she rushed away into the darkness. There should be a litter of kittens coming soon. She was surprised to find herself looking forward to the big event as much as Benuel and Fredrik were.

Once the door was locked tight again, she decided a hot cup of chocolate would help her sleep and got busy pouring milk into a pan. On impulse she grabbed one of her son's favorite oatmeal cookies before settling into the overstuffed chair in the living room with her steaming cup.

Content to read the Bible, she leafed through until she found her marker at Romans 8:28.

And we know that all things work together for good to them that love God, to them who are the called according to his purpose.

She would have to wait for *Gott* to show her His path for her and Benuel's life. She continued to read.

For whom he did foreknow, he also did predestinate to be conformed to the image of his Son, that he might be the firstborn among many brethren.

Her eyes growing tired, she closed the Bible and meditated on the lines she'd read. All things *had* seemed to work together for good since they'd returned to Pinecraft. She just hadn't gotten used to the idea of being alone yet.

As the last bite of her cookie was shoved in her mouth, she slipped off her house shoes, pulled her legs up under her gown and robe and burrowed deep into the soft cushions of the chair.

Long sips of the hot chocolate soothed her. She set the cup down as her eyes began to feel heavy. Sleep wasn't far off. If she wasn't careful she'd fall asleep where she was.

The sound of Benuel crying roused her from her light slumber.

"*Nee*, get away," he yelled.

Heart pounding, her bare feet smacked against the wood floors as she raced to him and scooped him into her arms.

He fought her. *"Nee, nee,"* he shouted, pushing at her.

She turned on his lamp and spoke to him in *Deitch*. "It's me, Benuel. Wake up. *Mamm* has you. It was only a dream."

He blinked up at her, his eyes glistening with

unshed tears. "*Daed* was shouting." He used his hand to swipe at a tear threatening to run down his face. "I saw him hit you and you cried out."

"*Nee*, it was only a dream, Benuel. You see? I'm wonderful-*gut*."

"*Ya*, but I saw—"

"What you saw was a dream. I'm fine, look." She laid him back against his pillow and smiled down at him as she ruffled his tangled hair. "We are safe now. I promise you. We must never worry again. *Gott* is protecting us from all harm. Jonah will never hurt us again."

"*Ya?*" he questioned, glancing around his room, his eyes wide and round.

She soothed him, her hand gently touching his face. "We are safe. Now, close your eyes. I'll sing your favorite song."

She trembled as she quietly sang the "Father Abraham" hymn he'd come to love.

His lids closed, but she felt the shuddering breath he took just before he dropped off. Sobs broke from her. No child should have witnessed what Benuel had seen in his short life. She should have taken him and fled long before her husband died. The child paid for her mistakes. Others didn't understand, but she knew why she kept the boy close to her. She knew the horrors the small child had experienced. If only she could tell him that the man who terrified him wasn't his true father. But if anyone ever found out, she could be ruined. And so could Fredrik.

She rose from Benuel's bed, leaving the light on and the door open.

In her room she threw herself across her rumpled bed and wept for her fatherless boy who had lived through so much, for her tiny babies left behind on the hill and for herself. Would she ever find peace? Perhaps if she prayed with all her might at church tomorrow, *Gott* would erase these memories from both their minds.

Fredrik found it hard to sit through three hours of church without stirring. He surveyed the group of smaller boys in the row in front of him. Their hair all neatly combed in place, most sat quietly, waiting to be called forward.

Someone sneezed and he recognized Benuel Mullet as the boy turned toward the noise. The corners of Fredrik's mouth lifted. He remembered how it was to be a boy and long for the service to be over.

Fredrik heard Lizbeth clear her throat as a warning. The child had better behave or his *mamm* was going to do something about it as soon as church was over. The *kinner* turned back toward the front, but squirmed until he found a comfortable spot on the bench and settled.

Isaac Graber, owner of the bike shop in town, and his new wife, Molly, sang the last stanza of "Amazing Grace." He clapped his hands with the rest of the church, appreciating the good job they had done.

A hand gestured and he observed someone in a blue dress motioning the small boys forward. All eight of them, including Benuel, popped up and shuffled to the front of the church in a jagged line. They wormed their way across the elevated platform, sidestepping until they were a few inches away from each other. The lady in blue ticked off the beat of the hymn and on three they began to sing "Deep and Wide" and make motions with their hands.

Benuel Mullet's voice rang out over the other boys', his motions exaggerated, feet tapping. Two rows over, he heard Lizbeth groan her disapproval.

Fredrik's foot tapped, too. Awe transformed his face into a wide smile. The boy could really sing, his voice revealing a hidden talent much like Fredrik's own.

He remembered singing with the other boys in the community when he was Benuel's age. What an exciting time it had been, singing on the stage with everyone looking at him. Too quick, the song was over and the boys returned to their places on the front bench. Benuel's eyes twinkled as he spotted his mother in the crowd and gave a quick wave. He plopped down, causing the boy next to him to yelp. Fredrik couldn't help but grin. The boy was a handful, but talented and full of life.

Mose Fischer ended the service with a silent prayer and people began to file out of the church. Caught in the crush of people and *kinner*, Fredrik stepped behind Ulla and her husband, Chicken John, and followed them out.

"You coming to the potluck dinner in the park?" Ulla asked a moment later. "We're trying to raise money for a new family who's moved here from Beeville, Texas." Her eyes grew wide as she spoke. "A tornado blew everything they owned away. *Gott* was with them. Their neighbors didn't make it out."

He'd thought about going straight to the café to eat and then taking a nap, but the idea of doing a good deed and eating food Pinecraft's best cooks prepared changed his mind. His spirits lifted. "*Ya*, sure. I'll see you there." His bike was parked at the back of the church. He passed Lizbeth and Benuel and tugged at the brim of his Sunday best black wool hat. "Someday that boy's going to make you a very proud *mamm*."

She nodded and smiled. "*Danki*, Fredrik. He already makes me a proud *mamm*." She walked toward him. "You going to the meal at the park?" she asked, holding tight to her son's hand.

"*Ya*, I am."

She walked past him. "*Gut*. See you there."

His eyes followed her as she walked to her three-wheel bike and rode off with Benuel in the wire basket. He wished he was riding beside them, but he would see them there. Lizbeth may have put away her black dresses, but she was still distant and wore the look of a widow in mourning. He had to be patient and bide his time. Or move on and find someone else willing to become his wife. That might be the safer option.

With the exception of a strong wind blowing, the day was perfect for a meal in the park. Fredrik looked around for a couple of his friends and found nothing but families sitting together. He made his way to the long tables covered in plastic bowls, roasting pans and heated chafing dishes. The food line was already lengthy. He stepped behind one of his favorite elders and shuffled along. The man's wife and six children were in line ahead of him.

It seemed everyone had a *fraa*. Was he the last bachelor in Pinecraft?

He looked over and saw Mose, Sarah and their children at a long table. If he hurried, he might be able to find room to eat with them.

A big glass jar on the first table held the receipts for the moneymaker. He drew out a crisp twenty-dollar bill and dropped it in, thought better of it and added another twenty to the jar. If it were his family who'd lost everything... But it wasn't his family. He didn't have one.

Sometimes it seemed *Gott*'s will for his life was to live alone and lonely. Or that he had missed *Gott*'s plan by letting Bette slip past. Her decision to drop him for his best friend still stung and grieved his heart. If he'd fought for her, he'd have children by now, a home. But if Bette had been the one for him, *Gott* would have made a way. No, the problem was in him. He'd dated a lot in his youth, but hadn't settled down. He'd have to keep looking, find that perfect someone made just for him, if he hadn't found her already.

Hungry after the long service, he chose a thick slice of slightly pink pot roast and plump potatoes, glazed carrots and onions to go with it. Someone bumped into him from behind and said with a laugh, *"Dummle sich,"* encouraging him to hurry along.

Fredrik balanced his plate as he glanced back and smiled with good-natured amusement. Isaac Graber, with Molly at his side, trailed behind him. "You and the missus sang a fine song this morning," he said and speared a slice of bread.

"*Danki*. We do our best," Isaac said. "Your bike should be ready to pick up by tomorrow."

Fredrik laughed. "*Gut*, I was hoping you'd say that. Mose said if I keep driving in on that scooter he's going to fire me. I keep falling off since I got it back from the shop last week." Fredrik laughed as he scooped a couple of pickled beets onto his filled plate, and saw there was no more room for bread-and-butter pickles.

Isaac nodded. "I was delayed a day by Molly. She had an ultrasound appointment. Seems we're having a *boppli* come early spring."

"Congratulations!" Fredrik exclaimed, stepping away from the table so others could help themselves to food.

Molly Graber beamed with excitement as they walked toward an empty table with him. "I think my *mamm*'s more excited than we are. You'd think this was her first grandchild to hear her talk."

Isaac grinned at his wife. "My *mamm* will be coming down in December with a couple of my sisters. We'll have plenty of help when the *boppli* arrives."

"This is wonderful-*gut* news. You are truly blessed, Isaac Graber," Fredrik said, placing his plate down on the table.

"*Ya*, sure. That we are." He motioned toward a group of tables under the trees. "Come. You are *willkumm* to join us at the long tables. There is no need for you to eat alone just because you're unwed."

Fredrik hesitated when he saw Lizbeth at the end of the mixed families table, her son sitting close to her hip. "Perhaps I should—"

"Don't be a *bensel*. Join us."

"You can meet my *aenti* Hilda. She's a matchmaker, and come to visit, but I'm sure she'll have time to find you a *fraa* while she's here," Molly said.

He picked up his plate, but his steps slowed. Ulla had told him her matchmaker sister was coming soon and could help him in his search for a *fraa*, but now that she was here a funny feeling went over him. He looked toward Lizbeth. Had he already found the woman he wanted as his *fraa*?

He muttered, *"Danki,"* but his eye caught Lizbeth looking back at him. She glanced away after a few seconds, but he'd caught the content expression on her face. She didn't need him in her life. She was happy the way things were. As long as she was mourning, she and her son were off-limits to him and the thought ate at him. Perhaps he should meet with the matchmaker.

Chapter Twelve

Fredrik slipped onto the bench. Two people down, Lizbeth watched him scoot in. She began to eat as if his joining them at their table was of no importance to her. He tipped the edge of his straw hat in her direction a moment later. She did her best to conceal the thrill tugging at her heart.

She was glad he sat so near. She might get a chance to talk to him, tell him how silly Benuel had acted when she brought home a glass house for his beloved frog. She tussled with her feelings for the handsome man a few feet away. Frustration brought a frown to her face. She knew she could be a good *fraa* for Fredrik, but what if the doctor had been wrong about her miscarriage? Was it her body's fault her *bopplis* died within minutes of being born as Jonah suggested? And what would Fredrik think if she told him the truth about Benuel?

She pushed her food around her plate, making no effort to eavesdrop on his conversation with Isaac, but his deep voice carried. He mentioned his work at the furniture barn and the fact he'd been working on the apartment behind her home.

Gracie Troyer, slim and pretty and one of Pinecraft's new widows, made it a point to stop by the table and say hello to Sarah. She asked what time the next youth quilting class began. Her eyes stayed on Fredrik as the women chatted.

Her daughter of ten or eleven flushed pink when her mother suggested Fredrik should come by and fix a few things that needed to be repaired around their house. No doubt her mother was more taken with the man than the girl, whose father had died a few months earlier.

Lizbeth knew her thoughts were uncharitable. The widow might have a genuine need of Fredrik's skills. But then the widow put her small hand on the back of Fredrik's fold up chair. Lizbeth took notice of the subtle way the woman's fingers brushed his shoulder blade and drew his attention back to her.

Ya, there was more than just home repairs on

the widow's mind. This forwardness was not the way Amish women behaved in Pinecraft. As girls, mothers taught their daughters to be respected for their virtue, and Gracie seemed to have forgotten some of her training.

Lizbeth dropped her head in shame, her eyes glued to her uneaten food. She had no right to think so critically about Gracie. *Gott* would not be pleased. Fredrik had been very clear with his intentions. He was looking for a *fraa*, and if she put up a hedge around herself, it was her own fault he was looking at Gracie with an interested eye.

Mose collected Benuel for a game of tug-of-war with the younger *kinner*. She waved the small boy off with a smile and reminded Mose to keep a close eye on him. Benuel was learning, but he still had a fondness for running off, forgetting to stay close in crowds.

"I'm told you've rented the *haus* my *schweschder* used to own."

Wrapped in her own thoughts, Lizbeth jerked around, unaware she'd drawn Hilda Albrecht's attention. "*Ya*, the *haus* is perfect for the boy and me. We've found contentment there." Lizbeth replied in *Deitch*, the language the woman was fluently speaking.

Hilda had been introduced to Lizbeth at lunch. She was visiting her older sister, Ulla, and staying at the chicken farm for the next two weeks. The older woman looked young for the seventy years she claimed. Hilda was nothing like Ulla, who was average height, a bit on the stout side, with an unkempt look about her, thanks to her unruly gray hair.

Hilda was no more than four foot ten, if that, and thin as a reed. Every hair on Hilda's brown head was neatly in place, her heart-shaped *kapp* starched stiff and pressed. Dressed in a navy church dress and black apron, she seldom spoke anything but Pennsylvania *Deitch*, with a sprinkling of High German added with authority.

Rumor had it she had been the local matchmaker in the Shipshewana district of Lancaster County for the past sixty years. She was said to be looked upon as a mentor for the young women in her community. Since her beloved husband's death, she'd taken up travel and often arranged marriages between the Old and New Order communities in Ohio and Indiana. Her visit here was to see Ulla, but it was evident she planned on using her skills of matchmaking on some of Pinecraft's single and widowed folk.

The corners of Hilda's eyes crinkled, her suntanned face a craggy road map of present and past smiles and frowns. Her eyes flashed with energy and a love of life.

The smiling little woman carried a small

leather-bound notebook everywhere she went, and was prepared to jot down a prospective couple's names as she saw similarities and possible connections. Lizbeth's pupils flared as she observed the little woman squinting at Fredrik and Gracie, scrawling something down in her book and then shutting it with a satisfied twitch around her mouth.

"Surely you must be planning on living but a short while in the house." Hilda turned back to Lizbeth and put a hand on her arm. "I assume you'll remarry soon. Benuel could use the firm hand of a father."

Heat stained Lizbeth's neck and cheeks and warmed her face. Surely this wasn't the place to bring up the subject of a future marriage for her. Not with Fredrik and Gracie sitting close enough to hear every word they were saying.

There had been a time, many years ago, when her quick marriage to Jonah caused local tongues to waggle. Since then she'd become a closed-off person, unwilling to discuss her past or present with anyone, even her *daed*.

She gave Fredrik a fleeting glance. Sunrays glinted off the deeper red tones in his hair. Shoveling food into his mouth, he continued to nod as Gracie drew up chairs for herself and her daughter and spoke to him in muted tones. He seemed interested in what she had to say.

Pen in hand, Hilda scribbled another notation in her book, her eyes glinting with something akin to mischief. "You've known Fredrik Lapp a long time?"

Lizbeth's eyes darted Fredrik's way again. Surely Hilda didn't consider them a possible match? But hadn't she thought the same herself a dozen times? "*Ya*, we've known each other since we were *kinner*. Why?"

The diminutive woman laid down her journal and accepted a slice of cake from one of the girls passing out sweets from a large tray. "This looks good. Did you make it?" She turned to Lizbeth.

"*Nee*, not me. I believe it was Molly who brought the cake."

"*Ach*…yes. Molly." She took a bit of cake and looked around, surveying the people around her. "My niece already has a fine husband, with a *boppli* on the way."

"I'm sure—"

"Oh, yes. There will be many children for Molly and Isaac. And perhaps more for you, too." A line of chocolate icing was quickly licked from the older woman's top lip.

Lizbeth blinked. "I don't—"

"Oh, you will, my dear. It's only a matter of time until *Gott* moves the obstacles out of the way and shows you His will for your life."

She sipped at her sweating glass of sweet tea. A smile danced on her lips. "You want more children. Don't you?"

She answered, speaking the truth. "*Ya*, I want more." She cleared her throat. "I'd *willkumm* more children if it were in *Gott*'s plan."

"*Gut*. Then that is settled."

"Settled?" Lizbeth nibbled on her bottom lip.

"*Ya*, it's certain-sure settled. It's only a matter of time."

"For what?" Lizbeth's voice sounded strained to her own ears. She laid down her fork.

"For a new husband, of course. I have several prosperous men in mind for you. All you have to do is pick one." Hilda swallowed her last bit of cake and smiled, her eyes even brighter.

Lizbeth struggled to moisten her lips, which had suddenly gone desert dry. From the corner of her eye she watched as Fredrik rose with Gracie in tow, her arm tucked in his elbow as they walked toward the grassy baseball field. The widow's daughter and two sons trailed behind them. They looked like a family and Lizbeth didn't like it one bit.

Hilda seemed to scrutinize her reaction to the pair leaving and sent Lizbeth a consoling smile. Fredrik passed and smiled. "See you in the morning," he commented, and then shuffled along, his head turned, looking down into Gracie's upturned face.

Fredrik stilled his hammer. "*Gut mariye*, Benuel. What are you doing with that stick?"

Inside the backyard fence, the boy's head swiveled around, the stick he'd been poking into the ground covered in mud. He hesitated and then muttered, "*Rutsching* round."

"Fooling around or causing problems for something in that mud? Did you find something interesting?"

"*Ach, ya.*" The boy shook his head, dislodging a clump of caked mud from his ear. "Another *frosch.*"

Holding back a smile, Fredrik tried to remain as serious as the boy who had turned back to his task. "A frog, huh? I collected them when I was a boy. Is it a tree frog or ground frog?"

Benuel's hand came up. "*Is fattgange.*"

Fredrik put down the board he'd been holding and walked toward the fence. "You know it's not polite to tell adults to go way, don't you? It makes me to wonder if you're supposed to be staying out of the water. I'm sure your *mamm* won't like that mud on your trousers."

Benuel gave him a frosty look. "*Mei mamm*'s in the *haus.*"

"Can I see your friend?"

"*Ya*, but he's *mein*. You can't take him."

The old gate creaked as it opened and then snapped closed behind Fredrik as he stepped into the yard. He took two more steps forward and paused. "I wouldn't dream of taking your frog." He stepped closer. Lizbeth would throw a fit when she saw the muddy condition the boy was in. "I promise to only look."

"*Dummle sich.*" Benuel motioned for him to hurry with his hand. "He wants to jump out of the hole."

"Then you must let him."

Benuel shook his head in determination, his arms crossed against his chest in a defiant pose. "*Nee*, he's one of *meine freundins*."

Fredrik stood over the hole the boy had been digging around in. Lizbeth wouldn't like Benuel having another frog, no matter how much the boy hollered. He'd heard her say one was enough. "It's lunchtime. He could be hungry for a fat fly. Let's see if we can catch him later."

"I gave him a piece of *mein* sandwich. I want to play with him *now*." Bending at the knee, the boy used the stick to poke the muddy ground, searching for the frog.

Not sure what to do, Fredrik rubbed his hands together. The child was young. He didn't know he could hurt the frog with the stick.

Waiting for the critter to move was the best way to see where it had gone in the mire. "Wait, don't poke at him, Benuel. You could hurt him." He grabbed the child's arm, prepared to move him away. "If we stand here and watch, we'll see the frog's movement and be able to catch him and have a good look."

Benuel's expression hardened. "*Nee*, let me go. I want to see him."

Lizbeth had only been in the house a few minutes, but she still hurried and almost took a tumble down the steps in her haste. She knew she couldn't leave her son alone for more than a few minutes without some kind of situation taking place. Last time she'd turned her back on him to make his bed, he'd gotten into a jar of pickles and eaten most of the sour treats.

He'd been sick later that night and there was no doubt in her mind it had been the pickles. She'd gone to bed convinced she still had much to learn as a *mamm*. She had to be more diligent, set down stronger boundaries. One day he'd learn her rules were for his own good.

The wicker basket she carried through the gate was heavy with Benuel's damp trousers and dark shirts. She repositioned her burden, glanced up and then stopped in her tracks.

What was Fredrik doing holding her son's arm?

"Was tut Si hier?"

Benuel reached down, grabbed something out of the dirt and stuck it in his trouser pocket before he looked her way.

"Nothing's going on." Fredrik took his straw hat off, stepped away from the child and then raked his fingers through his sweaty hair. "I'm working on the apartment."

"The apartment is over there." Her brow raised, she pointed behind the shed toward the small structure showing through the hedges. "Perhaps you should explain to me what you were doing holding my *soh*'s arm in that manner?"

"Ya, sure. The boy was playing with a frog and I thought—"

"He might hurt it?"

"Ya. I didn't want Benuel to harm the poor creature and thought it best to pull him away." He massaged the back of his neck. "*Kinner* should be taught how to treat *Gott*'s small creatures when they are young."

"He hasn't had much training around small critters," Lizbeth acknowledged, setting the basket of clothes down and tucking a curl of hair behind her ear. Benuel had grown tired of their conversation and ran for the rope swing dangling from the old oak tree. "*Danki* for explaining it to him."

Fredrik's chin lifted and he smiled broadly. "I was glad to help."

He put his hat back on and walked toward the gate. "I'd better get back to work. I'm eager to finish the apartment by the end of the month. Northerners will be coming soon and I may want to rent the apartment when it's ready."

She watched him go through the gate and down the drive, her eyes misting. This kind of training was what a father was supposed to give his *soh*. She should have known Fredrik had no intention of hurting Benuel when he'd grabbed his arm. He'd been nothing but kind and considerate to both of them.

Her shoulders slumped as she turned away and bent to grab a pair of wet trousers from the basket. With a snap, she flipped the wrinkles out of the garment before pegging it on the clothesline. Her stomach churned. If only she could encourage Fredrik, like Gracie had done at the park the day before. But there were so many things left unsaid, so much that needed mentioning. She had to concentrate more on finding work instead of mooning over Fredrik Lapp, she thought, flipping out another pair of Benuel's trousers. She was in no rush to remarry.

Chapter Thirteen

The help-wanted sign in the bakery window was still there, giving Lizbeth renewed hope.

Careful that her hair was tidy and her *kapp* on straight, Lizbeth smoothed down her crisp apron over the soft blue dress Sarah Fischer had helped her make. She entered the bakery, a fake smile plastered on. She was nervous. More nervous than she wanted to admit.

She'd put on a good front when she'd left Benuel with Ulla, and hoped to continued her ruse of confidence until the job interview was over and she had the job. She needed an income. The independent streak in her insisted she find a way to support her son without her father, or the community's financial help. She'd do whatever it took to make a good impression on Lila Zook, the owner of the established bakery.

The fragrance of freshly cooked bread and sweet rolls assailed her, making her mouth water. She'd been too anxious to eat breakfast when she'd fed Benuel earlier.

She glanced around and found Lila, one of Pinecraft's finest cake decorators, waiting on a customer at the side counter. The busy little woman gave her a friendly wave and pointed to a chair against the wall, close to the door.

Lizbeth sat. A glance at the big round wall clock in front of her told her she was more than ten minutes late for her interview.

Benuel had thrown a fit when he'd discovered she was leaving him. It had taken far too long to calm him down and redirect his attention to a red bird in the back garden. With the promise of a cupcake if he behaved, she'd rushed out the door and down the street. Being late didn't paint a very good picture of her ability to be punctual.

"Lizbeth, come join me in the back for a cup of tea." Lila motioned to her from behind the counter.

Lizbeth nodded at Lila's youngest daughter, who was a year or so younger than herself. She made her way through the curtained door to a square table and chairs tucked at the back of the large kitchen.

"I'm sorry I'm so late. I had a—"

Lila poured two cups of strong tea and encouraged Lizbeth to join her at the table. "Not to worry. *Komm*, join me for a cup of tea and eat yourself full of doughnut holes." Lila laughed as she held up a plate of the sugary treats. "I felt too ambitious this morning and thought the whole town of Pinecraft was as hungry for doughnuts as me."

"Danki," Lizbeth said, taking a sugary doughnut hole and placing it on the small plate handed to her.

After a long pull of her steaming tea, Lila grinned. "You've come about the opening?"

The strong black tea was warm and refreshing against Lizbeth's dry throat. *"Ya.* I saw the sign and spoke to your *soh* about an interview."

"Gut, gut. I can always use a strong back to lift flour sacks and such. My own back gave out on me years ago." Lila studied her. "You're certain-sure you can lift fifty pounds, Lizbeth? You're awfully scrawny."

Lizbeth placed her teacup on the old table and sighed. "I thought the sign said you needed a day-shift worker, someone to ice cakes and make doughnuts."

"Ya, I did, but that job was snatched up by Rosy Hess yesterday morning. Luke should have told you." Lila gave an apologetic half smile as she patted white powder off her siz-

able chest. "But I still have that night shift position open if you're interested," she said and ate another doughnut hole.

Minutes later, disappointment weighed Lizbeth down as she walked out of the shop and down the street. She couldn't take the job Lila offered. The hours were wrong, and the job required someone who knew the ins and outs of a busy kitchen. She baked a good cake and her cookies were always a hit, but she knew nothing about making huge batches of bread and rolls.

Catching the glint of a sign in the window of Yoder's Pizza, she stepped down into the street and crossed to the other side, hope rising in her. She knew good day jobs were hard to find in Pinecraft, especially during the long summer months when things were slow and tourists few. Most owners used their *kinner* or *familye* to fill in when staff was needed, but there had to be something she could do to earn her way.

What her *daed* had said was true. She *wasn't* prepared for working, but she had no choice. She had to support her family.

Her nerves roiling her stomach into knots, she managed to order a slice of pizza and force down the cheesy triangle, nibble by nibble, as she worked up the nerve to inquire about the job opening.

Laughter coming from the back of the tiny restaurant drew Lizbeth's interest. Gracie and two of her young children sat on a bench, her youngest son's gaze glued to Fredrik's face as he punctuated his tale of Daniel and the lion's den with roars and gyrations.

The story was one of Benuel's favorites. Her *daed* told it to him often. The boy would roar to his heart's content as he listened, just like Gracie's son, Isaiah, was doing now.

A tear escaped the corner of her eye. It was her fault Benuel didn't have Fredrik to tell him tales from the Bible. Everything was her fault. A burst of jealousy clawed at her gut. Gracie had done nothing wrong, didn't deserved the harsh feelings Lizbeth had against her.

The woman was enjoying her time with an eligible bachelor, like any woman who needed a respectable husband to help raise her children would do. Lizbeth had no right to care who Fredrik ate with, whose child he told Bible stories to. She'd given up that right long ago.

She threw down her napkin and walked to the front of the store, determination in every step. If her fear of commitment kept Benuel without a father, the least she could do was find a job and provide for her boy all that she could. Even if it meant making pizzas all day alongside teenagers. She wanted to be a *gut mamm*, be someone Benuel would grow to be proud of, and she would. But what if no one would hire her? What would she do then?

Fredrik walked up behind Lizbeth and watched Ralf Yoder's expression soften as he spoke to her from behind the counter. "Lizbeth, if I had known you were looking for work, I would have saved that shift for you." He grinned. "I might have something later in the week, though, when the young scholars go back to school. Check back with me if you're still looking for hours."

She nibbled at her bottom lip as she turned to leave and bumped into Fredrik's arm. "*Ach*, I'm sorry," she said and then saw who it was. She slipped him a guarded look.

"Hello, Lizbeth." He tipped his head in greeting, taking in her blanched face. The woman had to need a job pretty badly if she was willing to work at a busy pizza café.

Her expression softened. "Hi, Fredrik," she murmured in greeting and walked away, through the door and out into the afternoon heat.

"Wait," he called out, rushing down the sidewalk to catch up with her. "You're looking for work?"

She nodded. "We must all work if we are to eat."

Fredrik took her elbow and moved her to the side of the sidewalk. "I would have thought your husband's family would have—"

Sadness clouded her features. "*Ya*, sure. One would think that, but life isn't always black-and-white." She hurried down the sidewalk, her long dress swinging with her quick steps as she hurried away.

"Wait! Mose Fischer is looking for a book-keeper, if you're interested in the job."

She stopped. Turned back toward him. "Are you sure?"

"*Ya*, as sure as my name is Fredrik. He told me he was going to start looking for someone today." He offered her a grin.

A smile of relief spread across her face. "Tell him I will be in early tomorrow morning if you would please." She turned on her heel and strolled away, her back a bit straighter than it had been.

Fredrik watched the woman walk the length of the block and then disappear into a crowd of tourists. He wondered about what she had said about her husband's family. Had they shut her out when Jonah died? Could that be what was making her so sad at times?

He went back into the pizza café and sat

down beside Gracie and her children. He surveyed the woman's happy countenance, her children's carefree manner.

"I thought you'd run out on us." Gracie's eyebrows waggled in good humor.

"*Nee*, never that. I had a good deed to do, is all. Now I've got to get back to work before Mose puts out the alarm that I'm missing."

"Sure, you go," Gracie said, her eyes smiling across at him good-naturedly. "The *kinner* and I hope you'll come by for a meal."

"Maybe soon," Fredrik said, and paused, taking a long sip of water from his frosty glass. He would be disappointing the widow, but he had made up his mind. She wasn't the one for him, no matter how friendly and kind she was. He wanted to find her attractive, someone he couldn't do without, but the sight of Lizbeth fighting so hard for employment dispelled all his doubts, brought clarity to his mind. She was the one for him and somehow he had to convince her or die of a broken heart.

Gracie gathered her *kinner* around her like a mother hen and made her way out of the restaurant, her smile gone. Was he so transparent? Did she realize he wouldn't be coming around anymore? Fredrik ran his hands through his hair and then placed his hat back on his head. As he watched her march along, she turned to wave goodbye, her eyes squinting in the noon-day sun. "*Gott* bless you, Fredrik Lapp," she said and hurried her children across the street while the path was clear.

He sought out Mose the moment he was back at the furniture barn. "I think I've found you a bookkeeper."

Sandpapering down a leg for an *Englischer* order, Mose paused. "*Gut*, I had no interest in searching. Everyone I know is as bad with numbers as I am, yourself included." He laughed when Fredrik frowned. "I remember hearing about you cheating at school and still getting the answer wrong when you were in the eighth grade."

"*Ya*, well. Lizbeth Mullet won't get the answers wrong. When I cheated off her pages I always got good marks," he said, teasing. He hung up his hat on the office nail and headed toward the back with Mose. "She said to tell you she'd be in to see you first thing in the morning."

"I thought your lunch was with Gracie," Mose questioned, his brows raised.

"It was, but Lizbeth happened to come in."

Mose nodded. "You think Lizbeth would mind doing some dusting while she's here? This place looks like we had a sandstorm, not a downpour yesterday." Writing his name in the dust on one of the newly finished dining room tables as he passed, he tutted in disgust and then opened the noisy building room.

"I think Lizbeth's prepared to do just about anything to keep from marrying again. She's independent and determined."

Mose looked at the day's schedule, grabbed a thick apron made of linen and wrapped it around his waist, his eyes watching Fredrik. "But you're not giving up, are you? I've seen the way you look at her."

Fredrik selected an order to fill and grabbed a matching apron from the hook. "We're just friends, but I wouldn't be brokenhearted if it turned into something more," he admitted with a playful smile.

"You'll have to be patient as you approach, Fredrik. I've seen the look in her eyes around men. That husband of hers did something bad, abused her in some way. She used to be strong spirited, ready to take on the world. Now she's as skittish as a colt not yet broke in."

Fredrik nodded. "I've seen it, too. I'm willing to wait, as long as I see there is hope."

"You may have a long wait," Mose told him, flipping on the noisy sander and going to work on forming a table leg.

Busy working with his hands, Fredrik's mind

went back to the first day Lizbeth and Benuel came back to Pinecraft. Perhaps it wasn't just the near wreck that had her hands shaking when she'd rolled him over in the street. Perhaps she'd already been scared by something or someone. Had her husband's family made threats? She said they'd given her nothing to start out fresh. He'd heard rumors about some of the Old Order Amish in Ohio. Strict Ordnung rules didn't begin to describe the rigid way they lived.

Anger pushed at him, bunching up his muscles, making his heart hammer. She'd had a haunted look on her face that day. The boy had seemed on edge, too, and had jumped at every noise. If *Gott* gave him an opportunity, he'd ask her about her life in Ohio. It was time her heartache ended. He'd make sure no one abused her and Benuel again. If only she'd let him rescue her...

Chapter Fourteen

The next morning the furniture store door shut behind Lizbeth, the bell over the door announcing her arrival. The barn-shaped building with a connecting shop was large, but cool inside. It smelled of freshly cut wood and furniture polish.

Lizbeth struggled to pull her shoulders back and forced a smile. She wanted to exude confidence, but all she felt was dread. What would she do if Mose Fischer didn't find her qualifications acceptable and refused her work? She wrapped her arms around herself, saw an unfamiliar man approaching and adjusted herself. Her mouth went dry. She licked her lips, waiting.

"*Willkumm!* My name's Leroy King. How can I help you today?" The man strolling toward her was young and tall and unbelievably lean in black trousers, suspenders and a bright white shirt. His traditionally cut hair was ragged around his oversize ears. The tuft of straggly blond hair on his chin announced he was newly married.

With a nod of her head, she acknowledged him and then glanced nervously around. She knew Fredrik worked somewhere in the big barn, doing exactly what she had no idea, but she was glad it wasn't his job to greet customers. The last thing her already stretched nerves needed was a conversation with the man. "I have an appointment with Mose Fischer. At eleven."

"Hmm. He didn't mention anything to me. Perhaps you could come back in…say an hour, and perhaps he'll be in by then."

"He called and warned me he might be a bit late coming in, and asked me to wait for him in his office."

"*Ya*, sure. That sounds *gut* to me." He turned on his heel, headed toward the side of the huge room and then unlocked a small office door and flipped on the overhead lights. Fluorescent bulbs flickered and then exploded into a brilliant glow.

A cluttered old desk, computer chair on wheels and single straight-back wooden chair filled most of the room to overflowing. Several accounting books and a weathered box of crayons were scooped up by the salesman, allowing Lizbeth to sit down while she waited.

"May I get you a bottle of water, or some refreshment?"

"Nee," she answered too quickly and swallowed hard. She would have loved a drink of something cool after walking seven blocks in the midday heat. "I'm fine." She nodded, her throat so dry she almost choked on her own lie.

She wasn't fine. She was thirsty, nervous and more than a little afraid she was about to make a fool out of herself again. Who was she trying to kid? She was no bookkeeper. The closest thing she'd done to bookkeeping was help her *mamm* add up the proceeds from a quilt sale and divvy up the cash. She'd given the wrong amount of change back on her first try. But she needed the job and would do whatever it took to figure out the numbers with *Gott*'s help.

Working a half day after volunteering as morning cook for the local firehouse, Fredrik breezed through the open back door, his thoughts on the bride's chest he'd designed the day before. Today he'd build the model, line it with cedar and stain it a dark mahogany before showing it to Mose for his approval. He'd need to add some kind of short legs to the case.

He made his way to his workstation and then leafed through the latch fixture catalog. He may have to order something special for a wedding box like this. New brides were particular about what they brought into their new homes. They'd want the best. Hinges that would last a lifetime, like their marriages.

He whistled as he worked, his mind at last at rest. He'd had a hard time getting Lizbeth Mullet off his mind the night before. He hadn't missed the embarrassed look on her face when she'd hurried out of the pizza shop. She'd needed that job. She may not like him enough to marry him, but he felt more than a little interest in her. Lizbeth's situation reminded him of his sister, Ada. She'd had a difficult marriage and then was widowed early on. It hadn't been easy for her, either. He felt like he knew what the young widow was going through. He ambled into the showroom and saw one of their newest salesmen heading his way.

"Hey, Levi. Did a woman come in this morning looking for Mose?"

Leroy put down his dust cloth and glanced toward the front. "She did. I put her in his office to wait. I hope that's certain-fine with you."

"*Ya*, sure it is. I'll just go keep her company for a few minutes, until Mose can get here." He grabbed two cold water bottles from the ice chest and meandered through the showroom, admiring Mose's craftsmanship, as well as his own, as he made his way to the front of the store through a sea of fine furniture.

Through the glass window at the front he could see Lizbeth seated in the straight-back wooden chair, her legs crossed primly at her ankles, her hands nervously twisting in her lap. He slowed. Sadness clouded her features, made her look older than her years. Perhaps lack of money was her issue and this bookkeeping job would take away some of her depression. He'd talk to Mose before the man could make his decision on who to hire. Putting in a good word for her was the least Fredrik could do for Lizbeth.

When the door opened she looked up, hopeful. But then the color drained out of her face as she realized it was only him entering. Not the reaction he was hoping for, but the one he usually got.

Lizbeth looked pretty, even though her complexion was pale. He watched her try to act natural, smile normally, but she failed miserably. At times he suspected there was something about him that set the woman's teeth on edge, and he didn't have a clue what it was. Perhaps she just didn't like his hyperactive personality and easy laugh.

She couldn't still be holding on to her childhood frustration with him, could she? When they were younger, he'd kept his interest in her a secret as much as he could. And by the time she was old enough to step out with him, her *bruder* said she was interested in Jonah, who worked in the lumberyard, robbing Fredrik of all his hope. He still found her appealing, and would do whatever it took to convince her he was the one to marry when the time came.

"Waiting to talk to Mose about the bookkeeping job?" he asked as he placed the drawings for the cedar chest on the center of the desk.

She lifted her chin. "*Ya*. As I said yesterday. I have to work."

He stepped back toward the door. "You always were good with numbers in school. I won't be surprised if he gives you the job."

She toyed with a wispy lock of her own hair and tucked it behind her ear. Her fingers went to the ribbons dangling from her *kapp*. "*Danki*."

He stopped in front of her chair. "I could talk to him for you, if you'd like."

Her face reddened. "*Nee*, please. I don't need you to plead my case. I either get the job or I don't."

"*Ya*. Sure. I understand. You want to get the position on your own merit."

He watched as her hands squeezed into fists, her knuckles turning white. She was stressed about interviewing for the job. He handed her a bottle of water and kept one for himself. "I best be getting back to work now. I'll pray you get the job."

He thought he heard her mutter that she needed all the prayers she could get, but when he glanced back at her she was relaxed against the chair and leafing through a furniture magazine as if she didn't have a care in the world.

The next morning Lizbeth poured hot water over the last of the breakfast dishes and threw a kitchen towel over the tub until she could get around to washing them later. Benuel was in rare form this morning, getting into everything, crying over the least little thing. She needed to spend time with him, calm him down so she could finish her housework. Today *would* have to be Thursday, one of her busiest days of the week now that she'd accepted work from Mose Fischer.

She had the first set of furniture barn's books to work on, but that would have to wait until later this evening, when Benuel was in bed for the night. There was wash to do. She sighed.

Wash day had never been her favorite day of the week, but Benuel's swelling clothes basket needed her attention and she'd just heard on the radio that a line of thundershowers was approaching from the Gulf of Mexico and bringing torrential rains with it.

A knock came on the front door. In a rush, she glanced in on Benuel. He sat at the coffee table, scribbling his name onto a piece of drawing paper. Stretched out in front of him, his restless feet rocked back and forth as he concentrated on forming each letter of his name with precision. She frowned at the thought of his pensive expression as she hurried to the door. She peeked out the sheer curtain.

Fredrik stood at the front door as he did many mornings, his head turned toward the pink rosebushes at the side of the porch.

She bit her lip and stepped out of sight. What should she do? Open the door and have to deal with another one of his repair projects, or pretend to be out?

Consternation crossed her face. She wished she could ignore his knock. Being around him made her like him more, put him in her thoughts the whole day and into the night.

Without giving herself a moment to consider what she was doing, she jerked open the front door and greeted him. "*Gut mariye*, Fredrik.

How are you this fine day?" she asked, holding his gaze. Her hand nervously tidied up the loose tendrils of hair cascading around her right ear.

She must look a mess. She'd been busy all morning, stripping beds and remaking them, cleaning walls where Benuel had expressed his artistic flare while she was distracted. A glance at her apron reinforced her dread. Grape jelly and a clump of peanut butter toast stuck to her bust. Her shoulders slumped.

"*Gut mariye.* I came by in the off chance I could install that new tile in the front bathroom."

He must have noticed her frown, because he quickly amended, "I could come back later if the time's not right."

She might have a day full of chores ahead of her, but she would be even busier the next few days preparing baked goods for the family dinner. Better to get the project done today and out of the way than dread it all weekend long. "*Ya*, sure. Today is fine." She opened the door wide and stepped back, allowing the big man through.

"*Danki,*" he said and stepped in. His work belt clanged as he strode toward the bathroom. No longer the tall, slim boy he'd been at eighteen, he'd filled out and walked with a certainty that spoke of self-control and confidence.

She hurried past him into the kitchen, and got busy with her chores. Her mind lingered on Fredrik for a few moments and then her thoughts moved to Benuel in the living room. He was being far too quiet, which was never a good thing with an ADHD child. With a sense of urgency in her steps, she hurried through the entry hall and into the front room of the house. Benuel stood on a stool on one foot, his thin body plastered flat against the corner wall.

"Was isht?"

"Fredrik is here," he said in a whisper.

"*Ya*, he is, but you have nothing to be afraid of." She took him by the hand and encouraged him off the stool. "He's putting in new tiles for the bathroom. Isn't that nice?"

"He tried to take my other frog." He looked up at her, his eyes troubled.

"He explained. You could have hurt the frog and he wanted to spare it pain."

"I was trying to save it." The boy's eyes glowed with indignation.

She smiled down at him and ruffled his ginger hair. "*Ya*, well, silly *schnickelfritz*, he didn't know that, did he?"

"*Nee*, but he could have asked," Benuel said, one corner of his mouth hiking up in a grimace. "Can I have a cookie now? You said if I played quietly I could have one."

"Sure, I think that sounds fair." She looked around the room scattered with toys. "You tidy up in here and I'll have a treat waiting for you in the kitchen. *Yea?*"

"But what about him?" he asked and pointed toward the bathroom door. He ducked as Lizbeth tried to slide her fingers through his ruffled hair.

"You will be brave and walk right past him, or I'll eat your treat. *Komm schell*, or all the cookies will be gone."

Her skirt twirled around her calves as she walked out the living room door and then slowed her march. She could see Fredrik down on his hands and knees, unscrewing the doorjamb stripping. He looked so much like the young Fredrik she remembered, his knees always on the ground, flicking a glass marble through the dirt or digging a hole.

She smiled at the unexpected memory. Fredrik chose that moment to lift his head and glance her way. Everything around her slipped away. She was a young girl again, no more than sixteen. Old memories returned, stirred her heart. Long-dead feelings poured in, strong emotions held at bay. In that moment he was still her Fredrik, her secret love. Her affection for him had grown over the span of their childhood and had never died. But he'd walked away without even a goodbye.

She put her hands on her cheeks to hide the rush of blood suffusing her face. Nothing had changed and yet everything had changed. There was a tiny chance he might grow to love her, but once he heard it was possible she would never have more children, he would walk away and find someone else.

"Is something wrong?" he asked, pausing in his work, one eyebrow arched.

"*Nee*, nothing. I was just remembering."

"You looked so sad. What did you remember?" He braced himself up on his hands, waiting for her reply.

"I remembered you in the dirt, on your hands and knees."

He smiled. "If I was in the dirt, you were probably right there with me."

She shrugged. "*Ya*. You're probably right."

"I thought you might have forgotten all the good times we had," he said, his smile widening.

"*Nee*, I'm not one to forget."

Benuel rushed up and pushed her from behind, propelling her toward the kitchen and breaking the moment. "You promised me cookies. Remember?"

"*Ya, ya.* Your cookies are waiting," she said, her heart still beating fast against her ribs.

"When you're finished with your snack come help me work, Benuel. I need a good helper," Fredrik called out.

"*Mamm?*" Benuel asked, his eyes glowing with something akin to anticipation. The child was finally coming out of himself, daring to reach out to others.

"*Ya*, sure. You can help, but only if you do as you are told."

"Hurray!" Benuel shouted and hurried to the kitchen.

She shrugged and gave Fredrik a glance, her lips turned up in a wide grin. "I hope you know what you're getting into."

He grinned back and inspected her face. "*Ya*, sure I do, or I wouldn't have asked."

Lizbeth made her way to the kitchen and grabbed the full pitcher of orange juice from Benuel's hand just as he attempted to pour it into a tiny glass. Another mess averted. She smiled broadly. The man may have thought he knew what he'd bargained for, inviting Benuel to help, but he didn't.

The house felt different when Fredrik was in it. Like a home. She turned to wash the dishes.

If Fredrik picked a woman to court, Lizbeth's heart would be broken—again. Unless it was her. But there wasn't much chance in that.

Chapter Fifteen

❧

"Go back up there and wait for me," Fredrik said to Benuel, his finger pointing to the top step. A grin spread across Fredrik's damp, ruddy face. He lifted his straw hat and wiped sweat from his forehead with the sleeve of his shirt.

The boy stopped his fast-paced trek down the steps and froze in his ankle-high boots. "But you said I could help you."

"You are helping me by staying a safe distance away from these sharp broken tiles. We'll go back inside in a moment and lay the missing edge by the door."

His head dropping, Benuel pivoted and scuffed up the steps, then paced at the top like a caged lion, turning his puppy-dog look toward Fredrik. "Okay, but you won't forget to let me help. Will you?"

Satisfied the boy was staying put, Fredrik scored another tile on his pencil line and snapped the stone. "*Nee*, I won't forget my promise. You're my helper." He turned back to Benuel and winked. "I couldn't have done the room without your expert help. Your *mamm*'s going to be proud of you."

A smile transformed his young face and crinkled the corners of his eyes. "She thinks I'm a *boppli* and can't do anything right."

Snapping another tile, Fredrik glanced Benuel's way. "Did she tell you that?"

"*Nee*, but she thinks it. I can tell." Benuel sat on the top step and stretched out his legs, his fingers tapping impatiently at his sides. "She's always telling me to slow down or stop having fun." The sides of the *kinner*'s mouth dropped once again.

"I was the same when I was a young." He gave a mirthless laugh. Being an overactive child had always gotten him into trouble. "If my *mamm* wasn't yelling at me, she was smacking my bottom for breaking something of my *daed*'s." He gathered up the pile of tiles he'd cut and started up the stairs. Lizbeth appeared in the window beside the door and then darted away as she realized she'd been caught watching them. Did the woman ever take a moment away from worrying about the boy?

Benuel threaded a hand through his damp hair, paused, but then rose and declared, "My *daed* is dead."

Fredrik paused, his boot inches from the boy's smaller foot. He patted Benuel's head. "*Ya*, I know. You must miss him a lot."

His face lost all expression. "*Nee*, I don't miss him. Can I open the door for you?"

"*Ya*, sure. You get the door and I'll carry the tiles." Fredrik observed the return of emotion to the child's face. Perhaps Benuel's comment explained why Lizbeth was so different now. Had her husband been a difficult man, a poor example of a father? Why else would a young, impressionable boy say he didn't miss his newly buried *daed*? "You see? We make a good team, you and I."

Benuel shouldered the door open and skipped inside. The smells and sounds of frying chicken made the kitchen once more a home.

Lizbeth continued washing dishes at the sink. The flush on her face and the clatter she was making washing the cutlery told him she'd heard the mention of her husband's death and was distraught.

The sun streaming in past fluttering curtains at the kitchen window made Lizbeth's butterscotch-colored hair look almost white blond, like it had been when she was a child. Recollections of a younger, happier Lizbeth flooded his mind. She cleared her throat and asked without turning, "Is he behaving for you?"

Benuel's arms dangled at his sides, waiting for the man's answer.

Fredrik knew the feeling of longing for someone to say something good about him. He'd always been so active he seldom slowed down long enough to draw much more than negative attention. He put his hand on Benuel's shoulder and squeezed gently. "Certain-sure, he is. Your *soh*'s a hard worker. I'm impressed how *gut* he follows directions."

Surprise spread across the boy's face, brightening his eyes, causing one brow to lift. "We're almost done, *Mamm*. Fredrik said I could help him mend the fence later, if that's all right."

Lizbeth turned on her heel and faced them.

"*Ya*, well. Maybe another time. Lunch will be ready in a few minutes and you'd best hurry and get cleaned up. I have errands to run later this afternoon. I hope that bathroom's finished by then." She touched the grout on her son's shirt collar. Her brow knitted as she glanced at Fredrik. Then she looked back to Benuel with a smile.

"Yeah!" Benuel clamored. "Fredrik can eat with us again, right, *Mamm*?"

Lizbeth's lips parted as her smile widened. "*Ya*, sure. I made plenty."

"I'll stay, but you have to promise to eat all your food or the deal's off."

Benuel scratched his arm, his eyes on his mother. "Even if there's no red sauce?"

Fredrik blotted his forehead with his handkerchief, the corner of his mouth lifting. "Even if there's no sauce."

The boy shuffled his feet, scrutinized his mother and then nodded. "Even if there's no sauce."

Scrubbing the last pan, Lizbeth glanced out the back window. The two of them were cleaning up the mess from the tile cutting, the sun glinting off both ginger heads. Fredrik called out directions and Benuel followed them to the letter.

Thrilled that Benuel was learning, she wanted to shout hallelujah, dance for joy. He was doing what he was told without grumbling.

She was making headway with the boy, but in a lesser way than Fredrik. Her mother's words came back to haunt her. *It often takes a community to raise a kinner.*

Her *mamm* used the words when Lizbeth was a teen and complaining about some old *aenti* telling her to be still or put her *kapp* back on while they were fishing or running through the ocean surf.

Ya. She'd prayed for *Gott* to send someone who was able to reach her boy, and that someone had been Fredrik. She shrugged, knowing she still lacked some parenting skills, but she was learning as she went, picking up on what made Benuel more agreeable, easier to deal with. She no longer felt so overwhelmed or troubled.

But aren't you considering your own needs over Benuel's?

Her thought came from out of the blue and penetrated her head like a lightning bolt. She braced herself against the kitchen sink and bowed her head, tears rolling down her cheeks.

Seeing Benuel with Fredrik today spoke loud and clear. She covered her ears with her hands, trying to keep out the truth.

It was time to tell Fredrik he had a *kinner.* Benuel needed to know the truth about Fredrik's connection to him. But what if she lost them both? Somehow, she could live without Fredrik in her life, but what about Benuel? Could Fredrik keep Benuel away to punish her for her secret?

What about Benuel's needs?

The thought vibrated in her head until she could no longer stand it. She had kept her secret too long. She would tell Fredrik the truth, but first she'd ask for her father's wisdom. She had to tell them both about that night in the barn.

She had prayed for *Gott*'s forgiveness and guidance all those years ago, but now was the time for the truth.

After Fredrik left, Lizbeth directed her son. "Please shut the door behind me, Benuel."

The heat from the deep roasting pan of beef was burning through the dish towels she used as pot holders.

"Benuel?" She braced the pan against the back porch's wooden handrail, looked around her and then down the driveway. Where could the boy have gone? He couldn't be far. He'd been in front of her when she'd walked out the kitchen door just seconds ago.

"Benuel, please answer me." Her voice went up an octave. She resorted to the Old Amish language he was so familiar with. *"Wo bist du?"*

Making sounds like a buzzing bee, he dashed up the steps, and then began to swarm around her, circling closer and closer. *"Komm. Schell, Mamm,"* he said. "I don't like to wait. It's a special *familye* day."

Placing the hot pan on the porch behind her, she took him by the arms and forced him to stand still. "Why didn't you answer me when I called?"

His brow went up and he looked genuinely surprised. "I didn't hear you call my name."

"Then how did you know to come?" she inquired.

A smile danced on his lips. "I got scared and came back for you."

"You must stay close to me."

"*Ya*, sure. I was just *rutsching* round by the front porch. I heard a frog." He gave a half smile, the deep dimple in his cheek spoiling her moment of discipline. Fredrik had the same dimple, but his had almost vanished with maturity. Shame. She'd found that dimple fascinating as a child. Pulling herself back into the moment, she shrugged and gave a deep sigh. "You are enough to test the patience of *Gott* Himself."

"Is *Gott* mad at me?" he asked, not looking the least bit concerned.

She slapped a hand over her mouth so he wouldn't see her wide smile. "*Nee*, *Gott*'s not mad at you and neither am I, but you must follow directions. What did I tell you just now as I opened the door?"

He glanced up at the sky, several of his fingers going into his mouth. "I can't remember," he finally said. "I think you said I could have a dog if I behaved at *Grossmammi*'s."

She took in the sight of him standing on the porch. Her only living child. For now, she would think only of Benuel. Soon Fredrik had to be told and she needed her father's insight on the matter of Benuel's real father.

Lengths of ginger hair protruded out from under the straw hat sitting at an angle on Benuel's head. He hadn't changed out of his dusty dark trousers, and she noticed he had only one side of his suspenders up over his arm. The other hung limp at his waistline. "Do you know how much I love you?"

He lifted his head, gave her a lopsided smile. "*Grossdaddi* said he knows a man with puppies in his barn. Can we go see them tonight, after we eat?"

"*Nee*, but I'll make sure your *grossdaddi* takes you to see them soon." She relaxed, smiled again. "Now shut that door behind me so we can be on our way. We can't have the *familye* thinking we're not coming to dinner." She snatched up the roasting pan and led the way.

He bounced down the steps and then grabbed the handle of his wagon as she placed the cooling food amongst the toys cluttering the bottom of the wagon bed.

"Is Fredrik a *schreiner*?" His question came out of nowhere.

"*Ya*, he's a carpenter. Why do you ask?"

Sunlight shone in Benuel's blue eyes. "I want to be a *schreiner* when I grow up."

"That's nice." Lizbeth made no additional comment. She was too stunned. "Let's get to your *grossmammi*'s house before dark falls.

An hour later she left Benuel with a plate of warm cookies Ulla had just pulled from the oven and walked out to the old farmhouse door, heading toward the chicken pens.

She opened the first gate into the large, noisy chicken coop and called out, *"Daed!"*

Others complained about the ammonia smell and noise of the farm, but they had never been a problem to Lizbeth. She had wonderful memories of cuddling down-covered chicks and laughing as she chased after her *grossmammi*'s pet hens who ran wild in the yard.

She'd been told her *grossdaddi* had started the farm back in the fifties, some years after Pinecraft's conception. Her *daed* had taken over the running of the farm when the leathered old man passed on to be with the Lord. What stayed with her now was the look of *Grossdaadi*'s weathered face and his winning smile that reappeared in her *daed*'s aged appearance.

Both old men were stubborn when it came to

their dedication to this farm, but they had vibrant affection for their families that couldn't be faulted.

The muscles in Lizbeth's chest restricted. Her father wouldn't live forever, just like her *grossdaddi* hadn't. *"Daed?"*

Short and squat, but full of energy and a love of life, Chicken John dumped the overflowing basket of leafy kitchen greens and breakfast scraps and turned toward her. *"Ya*, I'm here."

She'd been indoors most of the day supervising Benuel as he helped Fredrik lay the tiles, but knew the day had started out warm and then an unexpected morning shower had left the afternoon miserably humid. Her father's face looked flushed, his lip beaded with sweat.

He was getting too old for such vigorous work, but no one could tell him anything, not even the local doctor, who'd declared him arthritic and insisted he slow down. He'd probably never retire from his beloved chicken farm, unless Ulla could convince the headstrong old man he needed to turn the farm over to Lizbeth's *bruder*, Saul.

Her father took a colorful handkerchief from his pant pocket and rubbed his brow and face and then stuck the damp cloth back in his pocket with little regard.

"I need to talk with you, if you have time to spare," Lizbeth said.

His head bobbed. "*Ya*, sure." He motioned her back through the gate and latched it behind them.

"Let me wash up first and then we'll sit under your *mamm*'s apple trees for a spell."

Under the spindly branches of the adult trees, Lizbeth settled herself on the wooden bench her *grossdaddi* had made before she was born and tried to organize her thoughts.

She watched as the outdoor faucet sloshed water on her *daed*'s boots and then half smiled as he hollered when he splashed his face and neck with cold water.

Not sure what all needed saying, she didn't have a clue how to start this conversation, or exactly how much to reveal.

Moments later, his face still damp and shining, her father shuffled over and lowered himself to the bench with a familiar groan. He observed her for a moment and then spoke. "*Was ist letz?* You have important words to speak to me, *dochder*?"

Did he look older or was it the dread filling her that made him look too fragile to handle her news?

She spoke in a rush for fear she'd snatch the words back before she could get them out.

"Fredrik Lapp is Benuel's natural father." She looked up, saw his pale eyes widen and then glisten with unshed tears.

His jaw tightened. "I had no idea he was the one. You never said." He raked his fingers through his damp hair and then scrutinized her face. "Why are you telling me now, *liebling*?"

She took in the sight of her father's set mouth, the way his jaw ticked with fury. Benuel's conception was her fault, not Fredrik's. "Fredrik never knew he was the father of my child."

His pupils dilated. "*Nee*, it is not possible. He would remember."

"Not if he had been too drunk to stand up, he wouldn't."

John rose, towering over her. "He took advantage of you?"

Lizbeth's lashes fluttered, heavy with tears. "*Nee*, I was the one who took advantage."

"You?" He kneeled in front of her, taking her hands in his. "How is it possible, Lizbeth? You were little more than a child."

Her lower lip quivered. "I was at the singing frolic. Fredrik and Saul were on *rumspringa* and still sowing their wild oats. I knew Fredrik was drunk when he offered to walk me home. He had a flask of something that smelled strong of spirits." Her voice shook as she continued. "In the moonlight he kissed me." Her voice broke as she continued. "I led him into the barn." She lowered her head, her shame turning her voice into little more than a whisper. A tear escaped her eye. "The next day he didn't remember any of it. Nothing! I was still just Saul's little *schweschder*, someone to be tolerated."

"But—"

"*Nee*, let me finish." She squeezed her father's hand, saw the strain of her words on his craggy face and felt heartache like never before. "Fredrik left for his training before he and Saul were baptized. He was completely unaware he'd been with me, that we'd made a child together." She clutched her father's rough hands. "How can I tell him, *Daed*? He will hate me."

"Oh, *mein kinner*."

She wept openly, her voice cracking. "He remembers nothing, but shows an interest in Benuel's welfare now." She pushed back a wisp of hair from her face. "Once he finds out Benuel is his *soh*, that it's my fault he's missed out on the boy's life, he'll hate me, take Benuel away. Yet I feel *Gott* leading me to tell him. What am I to do?"

"There is nothing more to be done. You must follow *Gott*'s plan. Fredrik has a right to know. It must be you who tells him." Her father's face blanched. The look he gave her touched her breaking heart.

"I will tell him, but in my time." She would tell him. If she could find the courage.

Chapter Sixteen

Fredrik had eaten many meals at Chicken John and Ulla Schwarts's house, but he'd never felt more uncomfortable than he did this time. His affection for Lizbeth was growing and he knew she wanted no part of a new marriage. Not while she was still grieving the loss of her husband. He lumbered into the large dining room, shuffled his way around Ulla's feisty, diminutive sister, Hilda, and then stuffed his freshly washed hands deep in his trouser pockets.

As expected, Lizbeth smiled at him over the bowl she was carrying and hurried away.

He rubbed his chin as he watched her scurry between Ulla and Hilda. He couldn't blame her for not wanting him always hanging around. Had he been too obvious with his affection?

He'd told Chicken John he had things to do after spending his morning at Lizbeth's laying tile and then working on the chicken coops in the afternoon, but the old church deacon was stubborn and wasn't having any of it. His habit had always been to feed those who worked on his chicken farm, and they had both labored in the hot sun that afternoon.

He smiled as Ulla passed him. The sunburn on his face made his skin feel tight and painful. He'd meant to put sunscreen on this afternoon, but a call from his *bruder* had broken his routine and left him scorched at the end of the long day.

Chicken John came bustling in, took his seat at the head of the big wooden table laden with plates, platters and bowls of food, and pointed to a chair on his right. "Sit yourself there, Fredrik. Across from Lizbeth and Hilda."

Lizbeth grabbed the back of the chair farther down the table. "I'll sit here, *Daed.* Close to Benuel."

Benuel scrambled out of the chair he'd climbed into, crawled under the table to a chair next to Fredrik. "I want to sit near Fredrik," he declared to no one in particular. "He's my friend."

Lizbeth nodded her approval.

John's bushy brows lifted as he glanced at the child and then over to his daughter. "Lizbeth. Your chair is there, where you've sat all your

life. There's been enough musical chairs tonight. Two men are hungry at this table. We've
both had a long day of work. Sit."

She nodded, her face an empty canvas. "But
first I have to help finish putting the meal
on the table," she said and took a step back,
promptly bumping into Ulla, who carried a
steaming bowl of mashed potatoes in her hand.
"I'm sorry. Excuse me," she muttered and hurried off into the kitchen, her hands adjusting
her *kapp*, pulling at her ribbon.

A smile tugged at Ulla's mouth. "Leave her
alone, John. She's a grown woman with a child.
Let the girl sit where she likes."

"*Ya*, sure. I'm certain-sure you're right." John
leaned toward Fredrik and laughed. "Whatever
it takes to get a meal in my belly." He rubbed
the rotund stomach straining at his shirt.

"*Ya*," Fredrik said and glanced toward the
kitchen. Lizbeth entered the room, with Hilda
following close behind her. He redirected his
gaze.

In the past he would have wiggled his eyebrows at Lizbeth and teased her about obey-
ing her *daed*'s rules, but those days were gone.

The silent prayer, proceeded by Chicken
John's clearing of his throat, came and went.
Forks tinkling against plates covered Benuel's

muffled comments about the evil of all things green.

Fredrik poked a slice of roast beef into his mouth. He winced as he rolled his sore shoulders. He'd need a hot shower when he got home. Laying the tiles in Lizbeth's bathroom had pulled at a few muscles and stretching chicken wire an hour ago hadn't helped any. He had the grouting to do early the next morning and then he'd be working the late shift at the furniture barn. He'd be busy all day again.

He dipped his fork into perfectly mashed potatoes and rich, creamy dark gravy and swirled a chunk of beef in it. It was time to speak to Lizbeth about marriage. Time was slipping past. Mose kept reminding him he wasn't getting any younger. He shoved a forkful of green beans in his mouth and tasted bacon. He'd grown tired of hamburgers and chili fries. He craved home cooking, clean sheets and someone to share his long, lonely evenings. Someone like Lizbeth.

"This beef is wonderful-*gut*," he remarked to Ulla across the table.

She hooked her thumb in Lizbeth's direction. "Give the praise to Lizbeth. She cooked the brisket."

"It's certain-sure tender," he told Lizbeth and quickly looked away.

He'd caught her staring at him, her countenance almost dreamy, a silly smile playing on her face, the same look she'd given him when she'd turned fifteen and tried to kiss him on the small bridge connecting his parents' property and hers. Confused, he glanced back at her. She had turned a brilliant shade of cranberry red and was frowning now. What had changed?

He saw Ulla nudge Hilda with her elbow. The tiny woman redirected her attention from her plate to Lizbeth.

"You thought any more about me finding you a suitable husband?"

Lizbeth swallowed the water she'd been sipping. Her eyes glistened with tears from almost choking. She didn't turn her head, but replied with a firm shake of her head. "*Nee.* My life is complicated enough."

Hilda plucked a green bean off her plate and stuck it in her mouth. She chewed and then spoke. "*Ya*, but a husband would bring you stability and take over some of the burdens of raising a *kinner* alone."

"Pinecraft is a small tourist town. Even if I had an interest in a *mann* and wanted to get married," she said with a glint to her eye, "who would I choose at the end of summer months?" She smirked. "Elder King?" She tucked a stray hair behind her ear. "He's old enough to be my *daed.*"

"Your *grossdaddi*," Chicken John corrected with a smile, then went back to eating as if an argument wasn't going on around him.

"You see? He's old and there's no one else who's single." She dabbed at her mouth with her napkin and placed it back on her lap, seemingly satisfied she'd won the battle.

All eyes turned to Fredrik, with the exception of Benuel, who was making a mess with his red sauce and potatoes.

Fredrik looked up, saw everyone's heads turned in his direction and sputtered, "Oh... wait now. It's true. I am looking for a *fraa*, and stepping out with a few ladies of the community from time to time, but placing Lizbeth and I on a marriage list won't work." His forehead puckered. "*Nee*, you see. Lizbeth is still in mourning..." His voice trailed off to a whisper.

"Oh, *ya*? You think so?" Hilda's eyebrows rose. She licked her lips and took her notebook out of her apron pocket, ready to scribble. "Tell me. When did this romance begin? Perhaps we can find a way to work through any problems and settle on a wedding date."

Lizbeth set her glass down too hard, her eyes beseeching her father to say something, end this fiasco. "I don't think this is the time or the place to be—"

Chicken John rose to his full height and

dropped his napkin in his plate. "Enough talk about marriage and such at my dinner table. This conversation will continue another day," he boomed and then directed his gaze at Ulla. "I want my pineapple upside-down cake in the living room. I'm sitting in my favorite chair for a spell."

Fredrik put down his fork and shoved back in his chair. He cast Lizbeth a veiled glance, but her chair was empty. She'd left the dining room without him knowing it and taken Benuel with her.

Lizbeth hadn't slept well the night before, after Hilda's outburst about marriage to Fredrik. "Stand still, Benuel. You'll be late for your first day of school." Lizbeth caught the boy's wiggling foot, and then brushed at the tip of his scuffed black boot.

"I don't want to go to school!" He balled up his fists, his anger growing.

"There will be lots of *kinner* to play with and Beatrice will eat lunch with you." She'd prayed he'd be excited about his first day at school, not cross and uncooperative.

His eyes woefully sad, he sniffed. "You might forget to come pick me up when school is over."

"I would never do that. You know I'll be outside, waiting." She smiled. "Perhaps Beatrice can walk with us to school. Would you like to drop by and pick her up?" She scrutinized him, saw his anger building.

He dropped his head and scuffed his boot against the hardwood floor. "*Nee*, she's mean-spirited. If she says I'm a crybaby again, I'm going to hit her." His lips pursed.

Lizbeth's heart skipped a beat. He'd witnessed too much. "It's wrong to hit, Benuel."

"My *daed* used to hit you."

"*Ya*, but he was wrong for doing it."

His thin arms went around her legs and he hugged her close in a loving embrace. "I didn't like it when he hit you," he murmured into the folds of her skirt.

"I didn't like it, either. We must promise each other to never hit, never cause others pain. *Ya?*" An ache that never left tore at her heart.

"I want to stay here with you. Fredrik might come and he'll need my help."

"He's busy today. Don't you remember he said he'd be back in a day or so to grout the tiles?"

"But he might come and need my help." He scrubbed at his eye, making it red.

"*Nee*, not this time," she said, smiling down at him and running her fingers through his uncombed hair. He had Fredrik's hair. The color and texture was exactly the same. "We've got to hurry. Eat your breakfast and then comb your hair." She held him by his arms and looked down at him. "Will you promise to be good and do your best?"

He pursed his lips and then they spread into a big grin. "Okay, *mamm*."

As he hurried off, she felt dread building. Would his best be good enough for his teacher? The young woman in charge of the youngest children seemed too young and innocent to understand his difficulties. Had she even heard of ADHD, or learned what behavior the condition brought about?

She had to say something to the teacher about Benuel's anger, to give him a fair chance in school. "Hurry, Benuel," she called out, holding her hand to her roiling stomach. "Time's flying past."

Late-summer orders had slowed down to a trickle, leaving Fredrik with a half day's work at the furniture barn. He'd gotten off at noon, eaten a meal and headed to the apartment behind Lizbeth's house. He had plenty of time to apply a fresh coat of paint to the bedroom's walls and finish up the last of the small jobs that needed doing.

He revved the motor of his little scooter and

pulled into the driveway, watching out for the mama cat who often slept in a pile of leaves shaded from the sunshine by the eaves of the house.

Movement drew his attention toward the kitchen's side door. Lizbeth's actions were quick as she locked the side door and moved down the steps, her hair coming loose from her bun and flying around her face. "Is everything all right?" he shouted, his legs still straddling the bike.

She glanced his way, paused, and for a moment Fredrik thought she'd burst out crying.

"*Nee*. The school sent a runner to tell me I'm needed there." She hurried down the driveway, her long legs eating up the pavement.

"Is Benuel sick?"

She stopped and turned around, tucking hair up into her bun under her *kapp*. "They didn't say. Just that I should get to the school right away."

"Let me take you," he offered, patting the small seat behind his larger one.

He watched her battle good common sense for a moment before finally declaring, "I couldn't ride on that thing."

"They said quick, Lizbeth. Hop on. I can get you there in less than five minutes."

Still, she hesitated. "*Nee*, but *danki*." She turned and hurried away.

"Stubborn woman," he muttered to himself and turned the scooter's motor back on. Driving slowly, he caught up with her and growled, "What's important here? You getting to the school for Benuel or saving face by walking all the way and keeping him waiting for you? He could be hurt."

Her eyes flooded with tears and she began to weep, deep racking sobs. "I don't know what to do. I'm so scared for him."

Fredrik pulled his handkerchief out of his back pocket and thrust it at her, longing to hold her as she cried. He waited for her tears to slow and then said, "Wipe your tears and climb on."

She took the cloth, dabbed at her eyes and gave a bitter laugh. "What choice do I have? Benuel needs me."

Bunching her skirt up, she threw her leg over the scooter and moved up close behind Fredrik, her arms wrapping around his waist.

"Hold on tight." He tore off down the road toward the school. The woman would need a shoulder to cry on if something had happened to the boy. She needed a helpmate more than he did.

Reaching the school, he stopped, letting her jump off the back of the scooter. Should he come inside with her, help her deal with whatever had happened? But she ran into the school, forgetting he existed and leaving him to worry about the little boy he'd grown so attached to.

Chapter Seventeen

The next day was sunny and warm. Fredrik worked a half day at the furniture shop, grabbed a bite of lunch, and then headed over to the apartment to find out what happened at the school the day before and to finish a small project that needed doing before he could put the place up for rent for the tourist season. Feeling a little nervous a half hour later, he knocked on Lizbeth's front door. He continued to ask *Gott* for an opportunity to talk to her about starting a relationship, but realized the conversation may not happen with an inquisitive little boy running around.

"You're early. I didn't expect you until later this afternoon." Lizbeth grinned and allowed him inside.

"I only worked part-time today. Business is slow," he said, noticing how attractive she looked in the pink dress and crisp white apron she wore.

Her mood seemed easygoing, her smile flashing his way as he stepped over the threshold. Was this a good time to bring up the incident at school the day before? Wouldn't she have already told him if Benuel had gotten hurt? Still, he was aware she didn't want him hanging around her home any more than he had to. She was a busy mother with a hard-to-handle boy that kept her busy.

He spoke out of concern for the boy, his words hurried. "You seemed so worried about Benuel yesterday. Did everything work out okay?"

"*Ya*, it did, but Benuel was still upset when he went to bed. He and a boy had gotten into an argument and punches were thrown."

Fredrik nodded his head, understanding Benuel's need to fight. He'd fought the need to get physical many times as a boy, but his temper had often won out. "I'm glad he wasn't hurt."

"*Nee*, not a bit, but he got a good lecture from me this morning."

Minutes later, Fredrik thought about Lizbeth's comments about Benuel's fight as he mixed up a batch of grout the consistency of toothpaste.

Going back to concentrating on his work, Fredrik smiled to himself. Grouting had never been one of his favorite things to do, but sponging the glaze off the shiny new bathroom tiles relaxed him today.

Benuel sat on a small stool just outside the bathroom door, watching Fredrik's efforts. The smile on the child's grout-smeared face said he was enjoying his view of the new tiles and his day of suspension from school for fighting.

The boy leaned forward, his hands placed on his knees. Light tan grout dried between his fingers and dripped on his boots. "Can I help again?"

"Nee." Fredrik said the word too loud.

Benuel recoiled and shoved back his stool, his eyes wide.

"I'm sorry." Fredrik hung his head down and groaned. He knew any kind of uproar undid the boy's calm moments. The child seemed afraid of loud noises, sudden movements. After yesterday's incident at the school, Fredrik knew he had to mind his attitude with Benuel. Keep things calm and easygoing.

He scooted the large bucket of murky water outside the bathroom door and stretched out his back. "Look. Why don't you just watch me for a minute and then you can help me clean up my tools. That would be a big help."

"Okay, but you won't forget?" Benuel scrunched up his nose and scratched the side of it, knocking a dried clump of grout the size of a dime onto his mother's clean floor.

Someone had disappointed this child over and over again. He took in the boy's condition. What a sight. Benuel had more grout on him than Fredrik did. He smiled broadly, hoping to show the boy all was well. "*Nee*. I won't forget. Now you'll need to back up a bit. I have to come out and get the cleanup started."

Like on a spring, Benuel popped off the stool, wiped his hands down the sides of his dark trousers, leaving two light-colored chalk streaks. "You want me to carry the bucket?"

"Benuel James Mullet. What have you done to yourself?" Lizbeth stood drying her hands in the kitchen doorway, her eyes taking in the two of them and her floor. She glanced down at Fredrik, the look in her eyes accusing him of causing mayhem, much like Benuel had the day before by hitting a boy on the playground. "I can't believe you let him get in this condition."

She advanced and then took a step back. "*Nee*, I won't clean him. You do it. You're the one who allowed him to get dirty." She pointed her finger toward the back door. "Outside! The both of you need a good hosing down."

Benuel's gritty hand in his, Fredrik smiled as

he heard Lizbeth's laughter begin behind him. At times like this he felt like a father to Benuel, and he loved the feeling.

Lizbeth sat at the kitchen table for a moment, enjoying her cold glass of water and listening to Benuel shriek with glee as Fredrik hosed him down with water. A smile played on her lips. She tucked a strand of hair behind her ear and pondered the afternoon's goings-on. Benuel had been muddy before, even covered in pig trough goo when he was four, but an eyebrow and head full of dried grout topped anything she could remember.

The two of them deserved each other, she decided with a grin, and sat back with a sigh of contentment. It had been a long morning. A long week in fact, but having Fredrik around somehow brought order to Benuel's particular type of chaos, and for that she was grateful.

Fredrik yelled out in surprise. His muffled shout sounding something like "I'll get you for that, you *schnickelfritz*." There was no holding back the laughter bubbling inside her. As she laughed, a feeling of peace prevailed, soothing the inner turmoil she'd packed down until she'd been ready to scream.

Somehow she and Fredrik had become friends. Well, not exactly friends, but he was good for the boy and making a difference when no one else seemed able to.

Her hand bent under her chin as she contemplated the future. There would come a time she would have to tell Fredrik the truth. But not today. Was it possible he wouldn't take Benuel away? Would he understand her motives and forgive her?

She dropped her hand. Her eyebrows furrowed. Were thoughts of Fredrik's forgiveness pure foolishness? Somehow the truth would have to come out, and when it did… *Nee*, she didn't want to think about it.

She jerked as the doorbell rang and then rang again. Uncrossing her ankles, she rose and made her way to the front door. The shadow of a man showed through the foggy glass at the sides of the wooden door. Her *daed*, no doubt. It would be like him to check on her midweek.

With a grin on her face, she opened the door, and the friendly words she'd planned on saying wedged in her throat. With a powerful force of fury, she moved to slam shut the door, only to have it forced open against her.

"You don't seem happy to see me, Lizbeth," Ishmael Mullet said in his heavy Ohio Amish dialect. His hand held the door open. He stepped into the house and looked around. His clean-shaven face was moist with sweat from the hot summer day. "What a fine house you live in with your wayward *soh*."

Lizbeth avoided her brother-in-law's glance. He looked so much like Jonah. Memories faded in and out until she thought she would pass out. She couldn't make herself look back at him. Why was he here? It wasn't like him to leave his beloved farm during his busiest time of the year.

The palms of her hands dampened. She rubbed them down her arms and then intertwined her fingers behind her back to keep her hands from trembling.

Like a scene playing out in her mind, she remembered the man's parting threat the night before she and Benuel left Ohio. *You will be my* fraa *now.* His words had robbed her of breath. She knew what he wanted. Had he come to force her back to Ohio? A quaking spread to the core of her being. "Why are you here?"

He stepped toward her.

She stepped back and held her breath.

He moved past her, his long-sleeved shirt brushing against her. She cringed away as he strode into the living room. His presence brought a malevolence into the house that turned her stomach, sickened her. "I came to speak to you." He glanced back at her. "To extend a proposition that would benefit us both."

He removed his straw hat, turned on his heel. "Where is Benuel?"

"He's busy..." She fought for the right words. She had to get him out of the house before Benuel saw him. "He and a friend—"

"Yes. I saw his friend in the back garden. He's a little old for Benuel to play with, don't you think?"

"You have no right—"

His breath was hot on her face as he jerked her close, his hand tangling in the wispy hair at her nape of her neck. "I have every right, woman. You were my brother's wife. The bishop said I could have you as my bride, if I wanted you. You and the boy are coming back with me." His eyes narrowed to slits. His voice rose. "My brother was too easy on you. There will be no mouthing off from you or that boy once you're mine." He moved his hand to her cheek and caressed the curve of her neck as he spoke softly, his mouth twisting in a smirk. "You'll like being my wife."

"I'd rather die," she assured him and turned her face away.

He reared back, his arm ready to strike her across the face. Lizbeth's vision blurred, anticipating the impact to be cruel.

The blue color of Fredrik's work shirt suddenly appeared and then the tall, muscular man stepped behind Ishmael and pulled back the man's arm.

Her brother-in-law's face contorted with pain. As he was moved toward the door, a moan slipped from his pinched lips. Lizbeth watched as Fredrik held on to the man's wrist and thumb, his face calm, almost docile.

For an instant, Ishmael hesitated. Fredrik jerked up. A deep groan sounded. Fredrik had the man's thumb twisted at an abnormal angle.

Together the men marched to the door. "You will never come to this house again, to this town again. Do I make myself clear?"

Ishmael spoke softly, words Lizbeth couldn't hear, but she saw Fredrik react to them.

"I wouldn't if I were you. If you do, you'll live to regret it," Fredrik replied. "This community has a way of dealing with men who abuse women and helpless children." Fredrik shoved the man out the door and onto the porch. His baritone voice came out like thunder. "Make your way back to Ohio. You're not *willkummed* here in Pinecraft."

Lizbeth's teeth chattered; her body shook. She closed her eyes in defeat, frozen with fear. The violence she'd experienced for years had followed her to Pinecraft, her sanctuary. A sound behind her alerted her. Benuel had come into the house. Had he seen it all? He stood shivering, his face pale, tears running down his cheeks. Fredrik hurried back in from the front porch and swept the weeping child into his arms.

"*Nee*, don't cry, Benuel," he crooned. "The man is gone now and won't return. Your *mamm* is fine," he promised as he patted the weeping child on the back.

But she wasn't fine. She was defeated. She'd thought she'd done the right thing coming back home, but all she'd done was draw the evil here, to her *familye*. "Bring him to me," she said, not trusting her trembling arms to hold Benuel as she stumbled into the living room. She sat on the edge of the couch and held her arms out for her son.

Fredrik released Benuel into her waiting arms and then sat across from her. "This man was your husband's *bruder*?"

Through tear-dampened lashes, she looked up, so grateful Fredrik had been here to deal with Ishmael. "*Ya*, but he is not a *gut mann*, Fredrik. He always gets his way. His father is an elder and a powerful man in their valley." She lowered her head, her hands holding Benuel tight.

"You have no interest in Ishmael as a husband and father for Benuel?"

She shook her head emphatically. "*Nee*. He

came uninvited. He'd threatened he would find me if I ever left." Now was the time she should tell him about Jonah, how cruel he was, like his *bruder*, but she would not speak ill of the dead, not in front of Benuel. Perhaps someday.

Fredrik's lips thinned into a fine line. "I promise you, he won't bother you again. I'll call Otto later and meet with some of the elders. They'll make sure he faces punishment for his actions if he doesn't leave."

She reached out a hand to the strong man across from her. His touch was warm and reassuring. For a moment she felt safe from Ishmael, from his threats. "*Danki*, Fredrik. You have been so kind to us."

A corner of his mouth lifted. He squeezed her fingers, his thumb rubbing the back of her knuckles. "I'll be around when you need me. You can count on it." Affection glowed in his eyes.

She took in the sight of him as she spoke softly to Benuel. "You see, Benuel? Fredrik will see that Ishmael never comes back." But even as she uttered the words, she wondered. Would Ishmael give up? Would Otto and the elders of Pinecraft be able to control the angry man? A tremor shook her. She prayed what Fredrik said was true. That Ishmael would go back to Ohio and never return.

Fredrik patted her hand. "Don't fret. I'll keep watch in the apartment out back. If you need me, all you have to do is yell and I'll come running."

Lizbeth nodded. "*Danki*. I appreciate your kindness to me and my *soh*."

His eyes became bright. "I'm not being kind, Lizbeth. I care about you both."

She knew that he did, but she also knew she wasn't ready for a romance of the heart. If Fredrik wanted more than just friendship, he'd have to wait a long time.

Trying to keep life on a normal footing, Lizbeth took Benuel to school the next day, and then took herself to work. The bookkeeping finished, she moved mechanically through the big barn, skimming her dust cloth on every surface she could reach. She stretched to finish wiping the top of a tall chest of drawers and felt strained muscles along her right arm, where Ishmael had grabbed her.

The night before, her father assured her that Ishmael had been put on a bus headed for Ohio, but not before the angry man had spread rumors about her virtue to all who would listen. How dare he say she had promised to marry him? She bent to pick up a piece of paper off the floor.

Nothing Ishmael did surprised her. Nothing. From the day she had met him, he'd made attempts to inappropriately touch her when no one was looking. Finally, she'd tried to tell Jonah, but he'd laughed at her, called her names. Said she deserved what she got.

She began to hum Benuel's favorite hymn, the one she'd hummed the night before to lull the troubled child to sleep. Thankfully Fredrik had offered to sleep in the apartment and be close at hand if they needed him. She thought about his reaction to Ishmael, how he'd set aside his gentle ways to rescue them. She'd never seen him hurt a fly before this.

Tears welled up as she pictured Benuel in her mind. He'd still had a haunted look in his eyes this morning, even after she and Fredrik assured him they'd seen the last of Ishmael Mullet the night before.

She shouldn't allow herself to think of that evil man again, but had no idea how to accomplish such a feat.

She dusted off a beautiful maple bed and smoothed the display quilt out. What a blessing the Fischer family had been to her. Mose's offer of additional work hours to clean at the big furniture barn was a blessing. Sarah teaching her to sew Benuel's clothing and her income from the store would help her afford all the additional costs she'd have now that Benuel had started school.

Her brows drew together and she sighed. Had she made the right choice enrolling him in school? Ulla and her father seemed to think so, and she'd counseled with Sarah before making a commitment and filling out the papers that would allow him to attend the Mennonite Christian school.

Beatrice had been going almost a semester now and Sarah said she already saw a marked improvement in her behavior. But Benuel had been suspended his first day, sent home to think about what he'd done when he'd hit another child.

Why had he hit the other boy? Benuel had kept quiet about the incident, refused to tell her what had led up to the slap. He remained belligerent, but promised he'd never hit another again. Ishmael showing up at their door hadn't done anything but flare Benuel's troubled mood. Would he behave today or would there be another call?

Passing Joe, an older man who had recently been hired by Mose to work short shifts when the need arose, Lizbeth nodded her head and made her way to the back of the store. A quiet man with a rotund belly and short legs, Joe reminded her of the *Englischers'* Santa Claus.

He tugged at his long, fluffy white beard and nodded back to her.

The front bell dinged. She stilled her hand and glanced over. Her fingers tugged at her prayer *kapp* as Mose and Fredrik paraded in, both men drinking from cups with straws. Fredrik's eyes sought her out. He grinned her way as both men moved toward the workshop at the back of the building. His gaze lingered. Could he tell she was still reeling from the night before, her stomach still quaking? She smiled to reassure him she was fine and went back to dusting.

He'd spoken softly to Benuel before he'd left for the night and walked to the back of the property. His words were meant to reassure the quiet, troubled child. Had Benuel believed him? She didn't know, but the child had slept erratically next to her in the bed and cried out in his sleep more than once. He'd refused breakfast this morning, and when she'd left him at school later, he hadn't said much, just waved goodbye and walked into the building with his head low.

Her conversation with his teacher had given her a ray of hope that all would be well today. The smiling young teacher assured her she would be able to manage Benuel's ADHD issues now that she knew what was motivating his behavior. She would give him special consideration.

Lizbeth knew his attention problems would be an ongoing battle, but as he aged, his moods would mellow, his attention span lengthen. As a child, Fredrik had always been overactive and prone to silly moods, but his attitude had relaxed and changed for the better. He seemed able to cope with life's demands without a problem now. Like Fredrik, Benuel would never be a patient man, never be able to sit still for long, but he had *Gott* in his corner and her father around to help smooth out the rough spots.

Prayer brought her comfort after the day she'd had, but her nerves were still stretched taut.

When a man of Ishmael's coloring and stature entered the store a few minutes later, Lizbeth fought down the urge to run. Would she ever feel safe? If he came back she would have to take her *soh* and leave Pinecraft. And if she did, where would they go? *Nee*, she had to tell Fredrik the truth about Benuel soon. He would help keep the boy safe.

Her son's slumped shoulders and sad expression from this morning still troubled her. Maybe she should have taken him to Ulla's today. Like Lizbeth, his mind had to be on Ishmael's sudden visit.

She watched Fredrik move toward the back of the store. He was whistling and seemed happy with life. She longed for that feeling of contentment. Would *Gott* grant her the wish in her heart? Would Fredrik forgive her for keeping Benuel a secret? Would the man ever grow to love her as she did him? Her common sense told her probably not.

Chapter Eighteen

All caught up on his work at the furniture barn, Fredrik looked forward to the friendly camaraderie and distraction of his biweekly volunteer job with the fire department. Not fully trained yet, he often spent his late afternoons cooking at the local firehouse instead of fighting fires.

As it was located just blocks from his job, he had plenty of time to grab a quick bite of lunch and then ride over to Ringling Street. He parked between Les Cooley's big four-wheel-drive truck and the chain-link fence that surrounded the single-story fire station.

Glad to be out of the heat, he made his way through the side door and enjoyed the frigid air that surrounded him. Quieter than usual, Gabriel Torres sat manning the phone behind his cluttered desk. The dog-eared paperback the

Englischer was reading showed a gory picture on the front, with the mystery's title written across a bloody body on the ground.

Fredrik lifted his hand and waved. "Afternoon, Gabe. How's life treating you?"

Overweight, with the personality of a comic and the sensitivity of a mule, Gabriel Torres lowered his book and nodded. His smile was warm and welcoming. "Good. You?"

Fredrik laughed as he shrugged. "Can't complain. You guys been busy?"

"Not really. Just a small fire out by a couple of homes. You training today?"

"*Nee*, cooking. Anything special you want me to fix?" He was familiar with the man's ferocious appetite, knew most of his likes and dislikes. It would be chicken and dumplings or meatballs and noodles.

The big man licked his lips and grinned. "I wouldn't mind a plate of those Amish meatballs and cheesy noodles you make."

"You got it," Fredrik replied and then jerked open the swinging door on his left.

The kitchen was empty, the well-equipped galley cluttered with glasses filled with melting ice or half-drunk tea and cola cans. He was sure he had all the ingredients needed to prepare the simple, but filling, dish Gabriel asked for. There'd be at least a dozen volunteers and first responders coming in and out as the day shift ended and the night shift began.

The clean apron he pulled from the supply closet wrapped twice around his slim waist. He turned to face the long kitchen butcher-block island and picked up the small eraser board left by the day crew. His finger ran down the list of chores he'd need to cover before his shift was over. The meal needed to be cooked by five, but Tony, the kitchen manager, had noted that the pantry needed to be restocked by the day-shift workers as soon as possible.

To help out, he wrote a list of groceries needed for the busy firemen and left it on the counter for them to find. He welcomed any additional work. The tasks would help him forget about Lizbeth for a while.

Since she'd returned to Pinecraft, his thoughts had somehow become focused on her little family. Lizbeth still mystified him with her grace and beauty, but she'd changed.

He'd enjoyed teasing her as a teen, but his once-casual feelings for her had developed into something more intense of late. If she showed even the least bit of serious interest in him, he would ask her to marry him. He liked it when they spent time together. He already knew they were compatible. They could make a good marriage, if she'd just give him half a chance.

He smiled to himself, enjoying the idea of them as a family. He'd have a fine son in Benuel. Maybe they'd have children of their own, too. He knew he was ready to settle down. There wasn't a doubt in his mind.

Not patient, especially about something so important, he sighed with frustration. He had a suspicion Lizbeth might never be interested in him. Not in the way he wanted. Why hadn't lively, good-spirited Gracie been enough for him? The young widow seemed to enjoy spending time with him. He found her comely and respectable, but their courtship hadn't gone anywhere and that was his fault. The widow had a winning personality, several great kids, but there had been something lacking between them. Something vital to him. He had to love the woman he married and he didn't love her, hard as he tried. He wanted a *fraa*, a *familye*, but was it too much to want love, too? Even if it meant risking another rejection?

He took his straw hat off and then raked his hands through his hair. *May* Gott*'s will be done*, he prayed and washed his hands again before filling the dishwasher with glasses. Ishmael's threats had made a serious impact on Lizbeth and the boy the day before. He'd never seen a woman or child so terrified. If Ishmael was an example of what she'd dealt with in

Ohio, no wonder she wanted no part of having a man in her life.

The mystery behind her years in Ohio intrigued him. Was abuse the cause of her change in personality? It would explain why Benuel was so stressed. He was just a little boy, someone who should be enjoying his young life to the fullest. But instead the child tensed at every noise, seemed unable to fit into the Plain life around him.

Several men with smutty faces and dressed in lightweight gear ambled into the kitchen, all complaining they were parched and looking for cold drinks, something to snack on. They'd been fighting a grass fire just inside Sarasota County and needed to cool down quick.

"Looks like you had a hot afternoon," Fredrik commented as he poured the fresh lemonade he'd prepared earlier. He added ice to tall plastic glasses and cracked open a new bag of chocolate chip cookies. The men gathered around as he dumped the whole bag onto a plate.

Five dirty hands reached out and grabbed handfuls of cookies. "The fire wasn't the problem. It's the humidity," Will said, pulling out a chair and straddling it. He stuffed two cookies into his mouth and smiled as he chewed, his cheeks bulging. New at the station and still not used to working outside in Florida's harsh summer heat, the *Englischer*'s face was red and sweaty.

Caught up in preparing the meal, Fredrik half listened to the men's friendly banter. The hamburger sizzled as he dropped the breaded meatballs loaded with onions, bell peppers and minced garlic cloves into the hot skillet and waited for them to start browning.

He was putting water in a big pan for noodles when he heard Benuel's name mentioned in conversation.

Fredrik set down the pan and turned on his heel. "What did you say about Benuel Mullet?"

Abraham, a grizzled old Amish volunteer Fredrik had known most of his life, answered, "I don't know all the facts, but he went missing this afternoon. They're checking all the usual places. If he's not found soon we're forming a search party over at the Mennonite school."

Fredrik quickly wiped at his hands as he asked, "Where was he last seen?"

"I heard he was on the school playground. His poor *mamm* sure is torn up. My *fraa* called on my work cell and said she couldn't get the woman to stop crying."

The shrill screech of the fire alarm went off, sending first responders scurrying for their protective gear.

Fredrik turned the flame off under the pans and flew through the swinging kitchen door and into the heart of the building. Gabriel shouted the address and description of the building to the lead firefighter as he hurried out the front of the building.

"Isn't that the old Murphy building located a few blocks from the Mennonite school?" Fredrik asked.

The big man's chair protested as he swiveled and faced Fredrik. "It sure is. Why?"

A cold chill sliced through him. His breath became fast and shallow. "A five-year-old boy is missing and his school's a few blocks away. You think there's any chance—"

"There's always a chance. Let's get over there and make sure that building is empty."

Fredrik's hands shook as he suited up. He wasn't fully trained, but he wasn't about to wait around to hear if Benuel had gone in that building's direction. His brow furrowed as he tugged on high boots and ran alongside Gabriel.

He'd grown more attached to Lizbeth's little boy than he'd realized. His heart pumped hard and fast as he jumped onto the fire truck and they sped away. *Please,* Gott. *Don't let Benuel be anywhere near that fire. Keep him safe for Lizbeth. And for me.*

* * *

The crowd of people gathered around the old building grew, their bodies pushing in on Lizbeth from every side. She fought to keep her place at the front of the police barricades and yellow tape.

"Please, my boy may be in there," she moaned, brushing hair out of her damp eyes. Ulla appeared out of nowhere and slipped her arm around Lizbeth's waist.

"We don't know that, Lizbeth."

Lizbeth nodded. "*Ya*, we don't know for sure." Her voice broke. But he could be in the burning building. Bile rose in her throat. Someone had seen him on the property less than an hour before. The *Englischer* had said the boy had paused and looked at the building, but the man had become distracted and didn't know if the child had gone into the building or not.

She rubbed her hands up and down her arms, freezing cold and trembling in the summer heat. Why had Benuel run away? Had he gotten into trouble again at school or had Ishmael's return upset him more than he'd let on?

People were whispering around her. Pointing her way. What were they saying? Did they think her *soh* was hurt and unable to make his way out of the fire? The thought agonized her. Another shudder racked her body. *Benuel, where are you?* Her eyes fixed on the double doors of the construction building.

Otto Fischer made his way to her and took her hand, speaking encouraging words. The strength of the old man's firm hold bolstered her. *Gott* was with her. *His will be done*, she repeated over and over in her head until she thought she would lose her mind.

She glanced up at the sky, looking for some sign that all would be well, but saw nothing but black smoke and the worried faces all around her. Would Benuel end up in a grave like her other *sohs*? Would she lose him, too? Was this *Gott*'s punishment for her keeping her secret from Fredrik? Her legs buckled and Otto and Ulla held her up, their arms locked around her waist. *Gott's will be done. Gott's will be done.*

Three firemen rushed from the building, their flame-retardant suits bulky on their bodies. Plumes of billowing black smoke shifted with the wind, licking at the ground around them. "Did *Daed* check the yard around the apartment again? He might have found a way into the house," she stammered, coughing from the acrid smoke burning her throat.

"*Ya*, he and the men are looking everywhere." Ulla's eyes pleaded with her. "Won't you please come with me? We'll check the roads leading up to the park. He likes to play there. I have your father's work phone. The police are cer-tain-sure to call us when they find him."

"*Nee*, I've got to stay here. Benuel will need me if he's hurt."

"But you can't be sure he's in there, Lizbeth. He could be anywhere, safe and sound. Think positive. *Gott* is with him."

The building groaned. Lizbeth shuffled on the balls of her feet, trying hard not to fall as the crowd moved back. Two firemen rushed out of the building, one carrying a small bundle wrapped in a silver blanket. A stretcher was placed on the ground and the blanket unrolled. The blue shirt and dark trousers her son had worn to school covered the body of the small boy on the ground.

Lizbeth's heart skipped a beat, and she felt unable to breathe. She couldn't seem to swal-low as she pushed forward and rushed toward the crowd of first responders. With a breaking heart she cried out, "*Gott* have mercy on my boy. Benuel!"

Fredrik stumbled forward, dense smoke swirling in the sunlight directing him toward the big doors. Joy filled his heart. They'd found Benuel on the second floor, curled up and cry-ing, but he was all right. Thank *Gott* he was all right and they'd gotten him out of this furnace.

A board fell, and then two. Just behind him, Gabriel called out, "Make a run for it! The ceiling's coming down."

An explosion rocked the ground. Concrete and wood shook. The walls screamed, metal tearing metal. The darkness around him became alive with flames and falling rubble. Gabriel grabbed his arm, pulled him forward. The two men ran as one, stumbling over fallen debris. Something solid hit Fredrik and he went down. Unbelievable heat covered him. Pain pierced the side of his head. His world went silent and black.

Chapter Nineteen

A nurse in a white smock covered in yellow smiley faces pushed out a door down the hall. Her rubber-soled shoes squeaked as she walked with purpose, her gait long. The vibrant black color of her hair sparked under the fluorescent light overhead as she glanced at the chart in her hand and then surveyed the pensive faces in the cold waiting room.

Lizbeth half rose, her hands still grasping the arms of the uncomfortable hospital chair upholstered in cold, slick leatherette. Her mind was numb with fear and dread. She compressed her lips together and waited.

Tall and lean, the nurse made her way over and stopped in front of Lizbeth's chair. "Lizbeth Mullet?" she asked, her voice soft and inquiring.

"*Ya.* You have news? Is my boy…?" She stood to her feet and swayed.

"Calm down, Mama." The nurse smiled, urging Lizbeth back into the chair with her hand. "We don't want you passing out on us." Her pale brown eyes warmed with compassion as she patted Lizbeth's hand and said, "Your little boy's going to be just fine."

"The doctors are sure? He's breathing easy now?" She raked her hand through her tangled hair and tried to bring back a semblance of order to the falling bun at the base of her neck. Her *kapp* lay crumpled on the floor, forgotten.

The nurse chuckled, her easygoing demeanor calming Lizbeth. "He's breathing like a champ and calling for his mama. You can come see for yourself if you promise not to faint on me."

Lizbeth rose, but instantly saw an array of colorful stars swirling around her and slumped back down. She gave a mirthless laugh, annoyed at her own show of weakness. "I guess I'm a little shakier than I realized."

Taking the empty seat beside Lizbeth, the nurse sat a handful of files on her knees and looked Lizbeth over. "Did you inhale any of the smoke?"

"Some, but not a lot." She cleared her dry throat.

"Let me get you a cool glass of water and

then we'll make our way slow and easy to the pediatric ward. I'll have one of the doctors check you over after you've had a word with your son."

Lizbeth nodded and then looked up, her hand clutching her throat. Her concern for Benuel was replaced by her fear for the firemen who'd been trapped in the building. "Do you know... Did all the firemen make it out alive?"

The nurse scooped up the files on her lap and stood. "I haven't heard anything, but I'm sure someone on the floor can find out for you. Why don't I find a wheelchair for you and get you to him?"

Lizbeth rubbed her temples. "*Ya*, I need to see my boy, make sure he's all right."

A moment later Lizbeth gasped as she was pushed into her Benuel's room and saw him. He appeared small and frail in the twin-size hospital bed made up with glistening white sheets. A thin plastic tube came from around the side of the bed and supplied oxygen through a cannula positioned under his small nose.

"Benuel," she said and reached for his cold, limp hand.

The stench of smoke still clung to him. Someone had made an effort to clean Benuel's pale face, but gritty soot still lined his hair and brows.

His blue eyes blinked open and shut again. A cough racked his body.

Lizbeth twisted around. "Is he supposed—"

"Yes, he'll have a rattle and a cough for a while, but he's getting plenty of oxygen. The doctor must have given him something to make him sleep. He was a pretty sick boy when he came in."

Lizbeth shoved the loose hair out of her face and kissed Benuel's cheek. "And you're sure he's going to be fine?"

The nurse attached the file to the foot of the bed and turned to leave. "I'll ask the doctor to come in and see you," she said and opened the door. "You just make sure you're in his line of sight when he wakes up. That young man wants his mama." She chuckled and left the room, leaving Lizbeth with the sounds of Benuel's labored breathing and the steady beat of his heart registering on the monitors above his head.

Fredrik became conscious of a bright light shining in his eyes and tried to move. Pain fractured the light into a million shards inside his head. Someone close by groaned.

"Don't move, Mr. Lapp," a male voice said from a distance, but the words were muffled, distorted.

The dreadful groaning continued. Why

didn't someone help the man suffering? Fredrik tried to voice his concerns, but the labored effort forced him into silence. Where was he? Who was crying out?

Unfamiliar sounds encircled him. Voices became clearer, filled his mind. Words that made no sense sent him back into the tumultuous maelstrom of fear. The sensation of falling jerked him down into a vortex of sensations. Light became pain.

Something cool and comforting covered him. Somewhere a clock ticked the minutes away. *Tick-tock.* The suffering man became silent. Had he died?

Consciousness returned, layer by layer. Fredrik's eyelashes fluttered. He strained to clear his throat.

The man groaned again.

A surge of excitement filled him. The suffering man was in pain, but alive. He struggled to open his eyes.

"Mr. Lapp. Wake up, Mr. Lapp."

My name is Fredrik. He tried to correct the man speaking to him. He'd seldom been called Mr. Lapp. It sounded foreign to him…inappropriate. *I'm plain Fredrik*, he insisted. He heard no sound, just the all-encompassing groaning filling the air around him.

The darkness slowly faded and the light

around him brightened, compelling him to open his eyes. He struggled to sort out the black-and-white squiggles that became colored and then merged into the features of a man.

"Lie still, Mr. Lapp."

He was firmly held down. He began to struggle, hysteria building in his mind. *Why can't I move? What's wrong with me?* He sunk into the black emptiness coming for him.

Lizbeth spent two days in the hospital with Benuel, her bed the reclining chair in the corner of the small two-bed room in the pediatric ward. She hadn't gotten used to the antiseptic smell of bleach or the bad *Englischer* food, but she couldn't fault the brilliant care her cantankerous boy was receiving. His cough was much better, and the doctor promised he could go home in the morning if today's X-ray showed additional improvement to his lungs.

Ulla glanced at the clock on the wall. She knitted rhythmically on the navy sweater being made for Benuel. Her needles clicked as they created stitch after stitch. "Shouldn't Benuel be back from the X-ray by now?"

Lizbeth's leg was asleep and tingling under her, so she straightened it out and flexed her toes. She shoved her foot in her shoe and grimaced as the tingling turned to intense pain.

"The nurse said they'd be doing a blood panel, too. Maybe they took him to the lab," she whispered and pointed to the closed curtain around the other small bed, "instead of jabbing him here. Last time he raised a real fuss and scared the other little boy."

Her knitting forgotten, Ulla placed the needles and yarn in her lap. "Have you asked Benuel why he ran away yet?"

Lizbeth rolled her shoulders and pulled them back, stiff from all the sitting. "*Nee*, not yet, but I will soon. I don't want to upset him, but I think it was because of the fight he'd had with the boy at school. He was still upset the next day and then Ishmael came and scared the life out of him." She bowed her head. She should have noticed how stressed he was. She looked up. "I did ask him about the fire, though, and he promised he hadn't started it. He said he saw smoke and went to see what was burning and saw flames coming from the wall. I'm guessing it was bad wiring in the old building." She paced the room, wishing she could have gone downstairs with him. The nurses were friendly, but waking to find his bed empty had shaken her this morning. Would he run again? She prayed not.

"John suggested you take Benuel out of school until he's a year older, more settled."

Ulla picked up the knitting, checked her progress and plunged the needle in the last stitch dropped. She began to work on the sweater again.

"*Ya*, it makes me to wonder if that's not what's best for now." She was ashamed to tell the older woman she didn't know exactly what to do, but she would figure it out.

She wrapped her arms around her middle. If her *daed* thought school was too much for Benuel, perhaps she would keep him home with her awhile longer. His behavior had always been unpredictable, but she'd thought he'd been doing better than he was. She wanted to trust her own judgment but wasn't a mind reader.

Benuel's ADHD made changes hard on the boy. The trip to Pinecraft, new faces, new experiences, had shaken him, and then Ishmael had come and terrified him. She no longer trusted his teacher or the school to keep track of him. Not since the fire.

Fear gripped her as a new possibility squeezed her heart, made it skip a beat. Would there be a police investigation? Would they believe Benuel hadn't started the fire? She clenched her hands into fists at her sides. She had to pull herself together, not take on problems. She had enough issues to deal with. It would do no good to imagine situations that could change Benuel's life forever.

The door squeaked as it opened and her brother's face appeared, a brilliant smile lighting up his dark blue eyes as he asked, "Is it safe to come in?"

"Saul!" Lizbeth ran to him, threw herself into his open arms. "It's so *gut* to see you," she said, completely relaxing for the first time in days.

"And you." He pulled her away, surveyed her up and down. "Just look at you, little *schweschder*. It's *ser gut* to see you." His smile became mischievous, his eyes glittering as he lifted his hand in greeting to Ulla and then turned back to Lizbeth. "You've gotten taller, but not an ounce plumper," he said and dodged as she reached for his head, prepared to muss his light-colored hair as she always had as a child. "Still all bones and attitude, I see."

"No more than you." She threw her head back and laughed at his wounded expression. "When did you get in?"

"I drove the whole day and made it just in time to watch you sleeping in that chair last night."

"You were here? Why didn't you wake me, let me know?" Lizbeth tucked herself under his arm as she'd done a million times as a child. She was safe and content.

He brushed back the hair from her forehead and kissed it softly before he answered. "I didn't want to disturb you. The nurse said you hadn't slept in two nights, but thanks be to our merciful *Gott*, your boy is alive."

"*Ya*, they tell me he'll be fine and I can breathe again."

"They're still not sure about Fredrik," Saul said, tugging at his light-colored beard.

"What do you mean? Is Fredrik ill?" She touched her hand to her heart as she sat on the edge of the bed.

Saul eyed her. "Didn't anyone tell you? Fredrik ran into the building to find Benuel. The ceiling gave way and fell in on him and another firefighter. They're both in intensive care."

Her lower lip quivered as she asked, "What was he doing fighting a fire?"

"Someone said he volunteers a couple of times a week. You didn't know?"

"*Nee*. He never said anything to me about fighting fires." Shame engulfed her. She'd been so concerned for Benuel, she hadn't given much more than a passing thought to the firemen who fought the blaze and carried her son out to safety. *Fredrik is hurt!* Heat suffused her face. "Do they know what's wrong with him? Is he going to be all right?"

He took her hand and patted it. "They aren't saying. All I could find out is that the burning ceiling fell on Fredrik. Something must have hit him on the head, because he has a concussion." His face grew pensive. "He hasn't woken up yet."

A ripple of anxiety coursed through her. If Fredrik died he'd never know he had a son. She would have cheated him of that joy. Her body shook as she held tight to her brother and looked into his eyes. Somehow she had to tell Fredrik before it was too late. "I have to see Fredrik, Saul. It's important. I need to tell him."

"I know you want to thank him for saving Benuel, but the man's in no condition—"

Frustrated, she shook Saul's hand, beseeched him with her eyes. "You don't understand. I must see him. I never told him… Benuel is his *soh*."

Chapter Twenty

"No one from the fire department told me Mr. Lapp had a wife. His papers show him as single."

"What?" Lizbeth's head turned, her brows raised, as she tried very hard to look surprised. The lie her brother had come up with weighed heavy on her conscience, but she had to see Fredrik and tell him about Benuel before it was too late.

She plastered a half smile on her face, felt her lips quiver with nerves. "Oh, yes. Fredrik and I married recently. I was out of town and just got word of his accident." Shame burned in her, flushed her face. She hated to lie, but what could she do? Fredrik deserved to know the truth and only family was allowed into the intensive care unit. She did what she had to. *Forgive me,* Gott.

The nurse observed her suspiciously for a moment, shrugged her shoulders, opened the wide, swinging hospital door marked ICU and turned toward a door. "He should be in here…"

Lizbeth nodded, her body trembling as she slipped on the protective gown the nurse handed her and walked through the door and into a bright hallway lined with single-occupancy rooms.

She scurried along behind the stout gray-haired nurse dressed in a cheerful smock and matching pants, all the while praying in earnest. *Let Fredrik live. Please,* Gott. *Let him live.*

The nurse stopped at the last room and peeked in. "Here he is." She yanked a heavy green drape open enough for her and Lizbeth to step in. Dim, the room seemed like a shrouded cocoon of beeping machines and wires. There was a single bed. Lizbeth halted in shock.

Her glance first went to Fredrik's ashen face, then to the blood-soaked bandage wrapped around his head. She tried to stifle her gasp, but failed miserably. The pallor of his skin shocked her. "He's so pale." She'd never seen Fredrik vulnerable before. Her eyes shimmered with unshed tears.

"Most head-trauma patients are," the nurse

said and reached for his chart. "Have you spoken with any of his doctors yet?"

"*Nee*, not yet," she said, her voice wavering. She broke down, her shoulders shuddering as she cried.

The nurse pushed a narrow table away and assisted her to a gray metal chair next to the bed.

Lizbeth fell into the armchair, her head in her hands, sobbing. She hadn't told Fredrik about Benuel, and now it may be too late. Memories engulfed her, flashed through her mind. She and Fredrik as children, then their teenage years, when she'd hung on to his every word like it was gospel. Marrying Jonah out of desperation had wounded her heart, but the past five years had stolen all her joy, made her a miserable woman.

She'd sat in a chair just like this one before, watched the life of her tiny *sohs* slowly ebb away until there was no hope, their immature lungs failing them. The *kinners'* deaths had been *Gott*'s will, but not hers. She'd wanted to see them grow into men of strong faith. But Jonah's abuse had robbed her yet again. The doctors had said their early births hadn't been her fault, and implied the beatings she'd taken had brought on her labor, but how could she be sure?

Her fists clenched. Would Fredrik die this time? Surely *Gott* wouldn't take him from her, too. This couldn't be His will for Benuel's life, to not have a father. She needed a second chance. *Please,* Gott. *Give me a second chance to do it right this time.*

The nurse patted her on her shoulder. "Don't let yourself get too upset, Mrs. Lapp. Your husband's young and strong. Looks pretty tough to me. I'm sure he'll be just fine."

Lizbeth lifted her head and looked into the nurse's eyes, desperately wanting her words to be true. She saw concern and resignation there, but no clear hope. *"Danki,"* she murmured, knowing the woman had been trained to say whatever she thought a wife might want to hear.

"I'll give you a moment alone with your husband," the nurse said softly and left the room.

Lizbeth remained silent. *Please, Father. Don't let him die, too. I love him.*

Fredrik's lashes fluttered as he sluggishly awoke from the black fog surrounding him. He became conscious of incessant pain hammering in his head and then the weight of something heavy on his left arm.

He moved, the effort costing him more pain than he was willing to pay. He stilled. Instead he focused on his breathing, on the things he could see without moving, the sounds he heard. Close by a high-pitched beep matched the rhythmic beating of his heart.

Clarity came gradually. It was obvious he was in a hospital bed, his head without a pillow under it. A cylinder of oxygen hissed under his nose. Bright lights overhead caused him to wince. He momentarily blinked his eyes. He shifted his gaze and tried to refocus, but only managed to exhaust himself.

Questions bombarded his mind, made his head hurt worse, but he pushed for answers. Why was he in the hospital? How long had he been lying there? Was he badly injured? How did it all happen?

He calmed himself by gazing at the pale green curtain hanging from metal rings that ran along a silver railing. The curtains were so close he could almost reach out and touch them.

He heard the footfalls of someone walking, their shoes squeaking like basketball sneakers on a wooden court. He tried to call out, but his throat was dry. It hurt to swallow, to breathe. He coughed and then groaned. What had happened to him? Why didn't someone come to see about him?

"Fredrik."

He cast his eyes down toward the foot of the

bed. Lizbeth's face appeared. Her *kapp* was off, her hair in disarray. He could see that she'd been crying. She nibbled on her bottom lip like she had as a young girl, when she was in trouble and needed his help. "Lizbeth." He tried to say her name, but it came out garbled. He lifted his hand toward her. It felt unusually heavy and he let it drop.

Relief suffused her features, but concern quickly took its place. "*Nee*, don't move," she urged, touching his arm. Her fingers were cold against his skin. "You must remain still. You've been badly injured. Your head—"

"It hurts," he whispered and swallowed hard. *If only I had a drink of water.*

Sadness clouded her features. "I know it hurts. Please don't try to talk. Just listen." Her face contorted and then went blank. "I have to tell you now. Forgive me if I've waited too long, but I have to tell you in case—" A tear rolled down her cheek, and then another.

Fredrik knew it took a lot to make Lizbeth cry. Was he badly hurt? Fear gripped his insides. Was he dying? He closed his eyes and took in a deep breath. A spasm of pain gripped his chest, forced him to cough until his lungs seemed on fire.

Lizbeth came closer, bending over him. "Do you remember the night I turned nineteen? We celebrated by going to a singing frolic." She swallowed hard, drawing in a long breath. "You and Saul were on *rumspringa*. I don't know why, but you both came to the singing drunk."

He blinked his eyes. What was she talking about, this singing frolic? Had he and Saul been drunk? They had done a lot of crazy things on *rumspringa*. He sighed. Why couldn't he remember? Why was this particular event so important to her now? They went to a lot of singings when they were young. Dark circles of black clouded his mind, tried to draw him away from her voice.

"You took me home that night," she said.

He struggled to listen, to make sense of what she was saying.

"You offered me a drink from your flask." She paused, looking down at him with sadness shadowing her features. She sighed and went on. "Later we went into the barn."

"Nee." He forced the word out, hoarse and rough. He would have never taken her into the barn. *Nee*, he would have never done such a thing. He looked at her, their gazes meeting. A deep flush crept up her face. Had he? He searched her face again, saw the truth in her words.

"Benuel was conceived that night," she whispered, her expression turning somber. She turned her head away.

"Benuel?" The name came out loud and clear.

"*Ya*, he is your *soh*, Fredrik. I had to tell you before…"

But the black swirls beckoned to him, tugging and churning and then pulling him away.

Lizbeth observed the young *Englischer* couple rambling along ahead of her. Both dark-haired and casually dressed in jeans and knit shirts, they looked the picture of health and contentment. They were young and in love. She could tell by the way he grasped the girl's hand, the way she snuggled under his arm as they walked. Both were smiling contently.

They didn't seem to have a care in the world and she envied their joy, even though she knew *Gott* wouldn't approve of her jealousy. The Ordnung was clear, the scriptures taught to her at her father's knee concise and unbending. Wanting what others had would bring forth sin and death. She'd made enough mistakes. Took too many wrong roads. She had to learn to be content with her life and make do.

She tried to shrug off her self-pity. Today was a *gut* day. She should be happy. Smile even. Benuel had been officially exonerated from any blame for the fire and a homeless man charged. Fredrik's condition had improved enough for him to be in a regular room and Benuel was finally coming home after three long days in the hospital.

The night before, Benuel had finally talked to her and Saul about why he'd run away, how terrified he'd been that Ishmael would steal him away from her and take him back to Ohio, to the farm. He'd been ashamed of himself for hitting the boy in school, afraid he'd become cruel like Ishmael.

Her shoulders straightened with resolve. She had to set aside the past five years of her life, reignite her joy of living and push forward. But there was so much left undone. So much uncertainty in her and Benuel's lives. Her strength would be tested, but with *Gott*'s help she could do anything. He'd proved Himself a faithful friend and had been with her through her most difficult times while married to Jonah.

She picked up her pace and hurried along, hoping if she walked fast enough all the foolish mistakes she'd made would somehow be left behind her.

The halls of the hospital's children's wing were painted in bright and cheerful colors, the walls plastered with posters of friendly faces of smiling rabbits, but the smell of chemical disinfectant hung heavy in the air.

She paused two feet away from Benuel's door when she heard the sound of laughter coming from the room. She approached slowly. Her brother's deep laugh joined in with Benuel's high-pitched shriek of joy. Her steps quickened to the door. "Well, someone certainly feels better today," she said with a smile and did her best not to cry at the sight of Saul holding Benuel in his arms. "It seems you two have become good friends."

"Mamm!" Benuel wailed, his arms going out to her. "The nurse said I could go home today. Is it true?"

He coughed, but the sound disturbed her far less than it had when he'd first entered this place of healing. She was grateful for all the good care he'd received. *"Ya*, it's true."

Saul passed her son's warm body to her and smiled. "He's a handful, this one. I know only one other person who fidgets as much."

Their eyes connected for a brief moment and she saw his approval of Benuel, but recognized his comment was to remind her they still needed to talk about Fredrik and the role he would play in this child's life.

"I remember you being just as squirmy," she threw back with a smile, but knew Saul was right. Benuel was a carbon copy of Fredrik, down to his radish-like toes.

Saul grinned as the boy wiggled out of his mother's arms and grabbed the carryall from her hand. "Is this my clothes?" he asked, dumping the contents on the bed before Lizbeth could react. He stripped off his hospital pajamas. With all his might he pushed his leg into the pressed pair of trousers, lost balance and ended up a giggling pile on the floor.

"Perhaps if you slow down a bit you might be able to accomplish your goal, young *soh*," she admonished, but couldn't hold back the laughter bubbling up. Benuel had made it through the fire, his lungs healing so quickly even the nurses were amazed at his progress. "Here, let me help you this one time."

"*Nee*, I'm a big boy. I can do it." He so naturally slipped into Pennsylvania *Deitch*, his accent as heavy as Jonah's had been.

Lizbeth lifted her head and looked over at Saul. Tears shimmered in the tall, handsome man's blue eyes. "He is a handful," she admitted, "but we are working on the value of self-control and doing what is requested of us." She laughed when Saul chuckled at her words. "We are trying."

"Let me do that, old *soh*," Saul said to Benuel and lifted the boy off the floor and onto the bed. "You shove your leg in and I'll hold your pants."

"*Nee*, I can do it," Benuel repeated and pulled away from his uncle's reach. He struggled until he managed to get both legs in where they belonged. "I am five now."

"This little *mann* has a mind of his own and I have a feeling it will be many years of struggle before you reach your goal. But you're not alone. You have family and…others willing to invest their lives into Benuel."

Again a reference to Fredrik. She nodded. Saul was right. It would take a great deal of work and patience to deal with an ADHD child. She'd need all the help she could get. Especially Fredrik's.

As she watched Benuel's arms shove into the sleeves of his long-sleeved shirt, her thoughts stayed on Fredrik. She knew he was getting better day by day. Saul spent most of his days with the injured man and shared with her what he had seen and heard each night at the dinner table.

She'd almost stopped by Fredrik's room today, but dread had stopped her. She was probably the last person he'd want to see after what she'd done to his life. Being robbed of his *soh*'s childhood couldn't sit well with him. There could still be a high price to pay.

"I have a message for you."

"Ya?" she said and glanced over at Saul, expecting him to speak freely.

"Let's get one of the nurses to help this young man finish up with his hair combing and tooth brushing."

Her brow raised. "Someone?"

Saul nodded, his lips pursed. "I told Fredrik we'd be down in a bit."

Fredrik wanted to see her? She bit her lip. She wasn't prepared, but would she ever be? What he had to say could ruin her life. "Perhaps you should have spoken to me first before you agreed."

"I think you owe him at least a conversation."

She winced. *"Ya*, you are right," she admitted, her heart thumping hard at the thought of answering Fredrik's questions, listening to his accusations.

Occupied with trying to tie his own shoes, Benuel didn't seem to notice when she and Saul left the room a moment later. Lizbeth marched past the nurse's station, her mind overwhelmed with the next step in her life. She had to let Fredrik in. She had no choice, but why did she suddenly feel so relieved? Was it because Benuel would finally have Fredrik as his father?

Hadn't she wanted this for a long time? For

Fredrik to be there every time she looked up? Had she been fighting her love for Fredrik all this time, lying to herself? Was he the man *Gott* had created for her? She hoped so.

Chapter Twenty-One

The red-faced nurse flounced out of the room, leaving behind her simply put words. "Either you eat your breakfast of bacon and eggs, Mr. Lapp, or there will be nothing until lunch, and that's a good four hours away."

"Powdered eggs and rubbery bacon don't appeal to me today," he called to the slowly closing door at the foot of the bed. He suffered a fit of coughing for his rebellious words.

She thrust the door open a crack and shoved her head back in. Her eyes sparkled with determination. "And Nurse O'Brian will not be sneaking in vending machine doughnuts or Snickers bars today. No more Cokes. Not on my watch."

He grinned at her, feeling good about something for the first time in days. Getting a rise out of the old girl confirmed what he'd suspected. He was getting better, stronger, maybe even ready to go home.

Her face softened, becoming almost motherly. "Good food is what you need, Fredrik. Not garbage."

"I'd eat *gut* food, if you brought me some." His thumb jerked toward the uneaten breakfast tray. "I wouldn't feed this swill to a pig," he said and grinned mischievously around a cough. He added for good measure, "If I owned one. But *danki* for being so concerned about me."

Her lips set in a firm line. "It's my job," she declared and shut the door behind her.

His lips drew back in a full smile, his thoughts instantly going to Benuel. His *soh.* "My *soh.*" The words sounded natural coming out of his mouth. Joy flooded his spirit every time he said it. He was a father, the child's real father.

He'd felt an affinity to the boy since he'd watched the hyperactive child try to function in a world moving far too slowly for him. He knew the frustrations the boy faced. He'd dealt with racing thoughts, the inability to sit still for longer than a millisecond. Starting now, he would become a constant in his son's life. He would make sure the world made more sense to Benuel. He would make a difference, with *Gott*'s help.

Thoughts of Lizbeth cascaded in and were pushed away, confined to the dark recesses of his mind until he could figure out how he felt about what she had done. He didn't understand, but he would in a matter of minutes, as soon as Saul brought her to his room. He knew Lizbeth better than most. He would reserve judgment until he heard her reasons for withholding Benuel. He owed the mother of his son that much.

Fredrik shoved the tray on wheels away from the bed, threw back the sheet, then stopped. He eyed the hard cast on his arm, the bandage on his left thigh. He thought of the smaller bandage taped over the cut on the side of his shaved head.

He wanted to splash his face and comb what little hair hadn't burned off his head. Brushing his teeth with his left arm had proved difficult the night before, but it had been a hallelujah moment when he'd accomplished the task. He was glad he had the strength to get out of bed alone, to wait on himself for a change.

He hurt in places he couldn't see or touch, but he continued to make his way to the bathroom, flipped on the light with his cast and whistled as he accomplished his ablutions.

With his left hand, he combed through the dirty hair at the base of his neck and turned toward the mirror to see if he'd accomplished his goal. Not impressed with what he saw, he wiggled a singed brow at his own reflection and accepted his limitations. Using his cane, he ambled over to the comfortable-looking padded chair in the corner.

As he sat, his stomach rumbled. He rubbed it, leaned back and closed his eyes, picturing his mother's fluffy pumpkin pancakes. He turned toward the food tray, opened an eye and sighed. Perhaps he would try the pretend eggs, but only if he got desperate. For now, he was content to sit and wait for Lizbeth to arrive. Eyes closing, he laced his fingers across his sunken stomach and relaxed, his mind going back to Benuel. His *soh*.

Lizbeth felt her brother's hand on her back, his quicker steps urging her on down the empty hall. "*Ach*, there is no rush. We will get there when we get there."

"The man has waited six years to hear the truth from your lips. Don't you think you could speed up your crawl just a bit?"

She stopped and turned and was almost knocked over by her brother's bulk. "I know he deserves the truth. That's why I told him when I thought he was—"

"*Ya*. You told him, but not until you thought he was dying."

A couple strolled by and gave them a curious glance. Lizbeth allowed Saul to tug her by the arm over to the wall. "This is hard for me, *bruder*. All of this," she said, her lips quivering. "You've heard the truth. Every miserable mistake I've made. Do you think talking about this, especially with Fredrik, will come easy? He doesn't remember!" Lizbeth pulled away, her temper flaring. Too many sleepless nights of tossing and turning had made her short-tempered. She just wanted to take her boy and go home. Be at peace for a while before she had to explain everything to everyone, especially Fredrik.

Her brother pulled her into his arms, patted her back as he'd done a million times before. "I'm sorry. I truly am." With a look of concern, he explained, "I know you dread this moment, but think of what could come from it."

"*Ya*, that's all I think about, Saul. Fredrik could be so angry he'll take Benuel away from me. You know how hard it's been for me. The mistakes I've made since I've had the boy on my own. I can't expect Fredrik to say he's fine with everything and go on his merry way, making up his mind whether or not he wants to be in Benuel's life." A tear rolled from her eye. "I wasn't much of a mother when I came back to Pinecraft, but I've learned and grown. I haven't had the time to learn how to make the best of my boy's ADHD problems, but I will."

"Jonah is to blame for that. Not you. He kept you from the boy, allowed his mother to take over."

"*Ya*, but I should have protested more. Made a stronger effort to—"

"And been knocked back in your place? *Nee*, I think you did what all Amish women do. They obey their husbands, kind or cruel. Not so?"

"*Ya*, but—"

"There are no *but*s," he said, cutting her off. "You will go into that room with your head held high, tell your story, and Fredrik Lapp better give you the benefit of the doubt. I believe in you because you're my little *schweschder*, and I love you."

Saul hugged her close, and then pushed her along. "We will both be sobbing in the hall if this conversation continues." His smile was infectious. "Move, you silly *bensel*. We have much to do and Benuel is waiting to go home."

Placing one foot in front of the other, Lizbeth hurried along beside her brother, her hands hanging by her side. *Gott* would bring about an outcome and it would be His will for her life. She had to learn to trust and smile again.

* * *

Fredrik woke to the sound of his hospital door closing behind someone. He opened his eyes and saw Saul standing with his back to the door. Lizbeth stood in front of Fredrik's chair.

Pale and gaunt, she appeared as troubled as he felt and more than a little unsure of herself. He could only imagine what she thought of how he looked, with his bandaged body and blood-splatted hair standing up at all angles around the bandage wrapped round his head.

It was painful to sit up, but he managed it with as little fanfare as possible. "Hello," he said in a voice he didn't recognize. He coughed. His lungs were still healing from the smoke he'd taken in, but he could breathe now without wanting to cry out in pain. That was an improvement.

"You look better," Lizbeth said and looked down, their gazes not meeting.

"*Ya*, better," he said, not sure how to start this conversation without her help.

Saul opened the door and slipped out quietly.

Fredrik turned back to Lizbeth, saw her eyes opened wide. Was she afraid of him? Did she think him a monster, void of feeling? She'd lied to him, kept secrets best said, but he'd never hurt or abuse her. She was the mother of his *soh*.

In that moment he knew she was the woman

he loved with all his heart. He'd known his boyhood interest in her was still alive and well, but when had it turned into such a deep devotion? He didn't know, and he didn't care. All he knew was he had to listen to her explain and then tell her what was in his heart.

"Saul said you wanted to see me." She lowered herself to the straight-back chair next to the bed and sat, her shoulders back, ankles crossed. Both her hands clutched the fabric of her dress.

"I do." He paused as he coughed, and then wiped his mouth with the back of his hand. "I'm sorry. The smoke—"

She sat forward. "Don't apologize."

"Nee," he said and prayed for *Gott* to put the right words into his mouth. "I have been thinking…about what you said. How Benuel is *mein soh*?"

"I had to tell you." She worried the fabric of her collar with her hand and squirmed uncomfortably in the chair. "If you had died, you would never have known. Every father deserves to know he has a child."

He caught her gaze, saw the pain she was going through. "I'm glad you told me when you did. It made my will to live stronger."

He watched her relax, saw her hands unclench.

"I'm glad," she said.

"I'm sorry I took advantage of you that day. Sorry you had to deal with the reality of our *kinner* alone," Fredrik said.

She rose and slowly moved toward him, her hand outstretched. "But I was glad to be carrying your child. Didn't you know that I... I loved you? Since I was a young girl I clung to your every word, sought out ways to be around you." She knelt by his chair, her hand on his knee.

Fredrik shook his head, not believing the words she was saying. "Then why did you seem so distant when you came back to Pinecraft? You acted like the sight of me made you nervous."

The corner of her mouth angled up into a radiant smile. "You did make me nervous. You reminded me of how foolish I'd been. The mistakes I'd made." She dropped her gaze. "Every time I saw you with Benuel I thought of what could have been, what should have been."

He reached for her hand, rubbed his thumb across her knuckles. "Why didn't you find me, tell me about Benuel? We could have married. There'd have been no need for you to marry Jonah," he said and then added, "Unless you loved him."

She blanched. "*Nee,* I didn't love him. Not for a moment. At first he was kind to me."

"Go on," Fredrik urged, bitterly angry with himself for taking advantage of Lizbeth. She'd been so young when he'd left for training in Ohio. Only nineteen. He'd joined the church there, been baptized, courted Bette. His mind had been on his own life, not the life growing inside her body. Why had he forgotten such an important moment? He must have been very drunk. What a *bensel* he was. Why had she protected him like that? She should have sent her father to deal with him.

"I tried to find you on my own, but my father kept asking me who the *boppli*'s father was. Pressuring me. I didn't want you in trouble with the bishop, the elders of the church. You were finally getting your life in order, courting a girl." Her chin touched her chest. "Finally, my father paid Jonah to marry me." She blinked away the tears. "*Daed* did what he thought best for me, for the *kinner*. Jonah accepted the money after the marriage, promised he forgave the past and said he would be a real father to *our child*. I believed him for a time, but after we arrived in Ohio everything changed."

"What happened?" A terrible rage built in his gut, tearing at him.

"Jonah became abusive with his words and his hands." She turned her head toward the wall, her eyes staring.

"Why didn't you contact your father?" Fredrik demanded.

"I tried, but Jonah found out. I was punished, kept in a room, my arm chained to the bed like a dog. When my time came, Jonah's mother delivered our *kinner*. Benuel was taken from me at birth, only brought to me to nurse."

She turned back to Fredrik, her wide gaze showing her need for understanding. "I was seldom allowed to see him that first year. He lived on Jonah's parents' farm, miles away. I was only allowed to be around the child if I behaved. Obeyed Jonah's every word.

"But then Jonah died and I was suddenly freed. One of the women helped me get away with Benuel in tow. She understood what I'd been going through, what most of the women in that community go through. That day you almost hit Benuel was my first day home. I was still in shock."

"And I almost ran you both down." Fredrik felt a shiver go through him.

"*Ya*, you did."

"I must have been a thorn in your flesh."

"Not a thorn for certain-sure."

"Why did you protect me, Lizbeth? You should have—"

"*Nee*, you can't say what I should have done. You didn't love me. Our love was one-sided.

That night happened because I wanted it to. You have no blame in this. You didn't even remember."

"You have to know that fact doesn't make me feel any better. I had strong feelings for you. I should have realized something like this could happen. But you were still so young. I thought if I waited…"

"You said you loved me that night," she said, her eyes damp with tears. She studied his face.

Fredrik drew her to him, with his good arm wrapping around her waist. "I did love you, silly woman. Can't you see it in my eyes?"

Lizbeth's lips lifted in a perfect bow, her joy shining in her blue eyes. "I do see the love, Fredrik. For the first time I see true love and it is almost more than I can manage. I want so badly for you to kiss me."

Fredrik lowered his head, his lips touching her, pressing down until he could no longer breathe and had to pull away. "You take my breath away, Lizbeth."

"I think the smoke did that," she purred, snuggling close.

"*Nee*, it was you, my love."

Epilogue

A Christmas wedding was more than Lizbeth had dared hope for, but for the past few months Fredrik had seemed set on making her every dream come true.

He wore his best blue shirt and trousers, his hair trimmed expertly around his ears. The shade of his blue eyes darkened as he held her gaze and spoke his vows of unwavering love to her. "You are my one true love. I will be devoted to you and Benuel till my last breath."

A smile played on her lips as they were announced man and wife. *Thank You,* Gott. They were finally a *familye.*

"*Ya,* this is the part of the wedding I like best," Otto Fischer said and chortled as he wedged himself between Fredrik and Lizbeth on the church platform. "Congregation… I take great pleasure in introducing to you… Fredrik and Lizbeth Lapp. May *Gott*'s blessings rest upon them and, in His benevolent mercy, allow all their problems to be little ones. Now let's eat! A man grows hungry after such a long service."

Benuel bounded from the bench at the side of the church and shouted to his mother, "Is he finally my *daed* now?"

Lizbeth's tears of joy rolled down her cheeks as Fredrik picked the small boy up in his arms and carried him out the church door, declaring emphatically, "*Ya*, I am your *daed*, Benuel. We have much to talk about, you and I."

Lizbeth hurried along after her two favorite men and sat on the same wooden bench well hidden under the old oak tree draped with moss at the side of the church.

Benuel glanced at his mother's face, saw her glistening tears and frowned, his rusty brows lowering. "Are you sad, *Mamm*? I thought you wanted to marry Fredrik?"

"I did. I do." She chuckled, brushing away her tears. "These are tears of joy. I love being married to your father."

"My friend Joseph said Fredrik's not really my *daed*," Benuel said, scratching at the stiff collar of his blue church shirt. "You are my *daed*, right?" he asked, looking at Fredrik for confirmation.

"I am, and have always been, Benuel. For a time, Jonah took care of you as a substitute *daed*, but I have always been your real father. I'm sorry I couldn't always be with you to protect and love you."

"You were my *daed* when I was a baby?" Benuel asked, his eyes growing round with wonder.

Lizbeth held her breath, her eyes seeking Fredrik's face. She smiled tenderly, looking into his blue-eyed gaze and thanking him for loving her enough to make this transition easier for Benuel. The boy was still too young to completely understand, but given time and patience, he would recognize life wasn't always cut-and-dried, didn't always go the way it should.

Fredrik sat the child on his lap, hugged him close. "I was your *daed* when you were born, but your mother couldn't find me. I had gone far away and she was alone and needed someone. Jonah promised to take care of you and your mother until she found me."

Benuel looked up, his eyes misty, the edges of his small mouth turned down. "Jonah was mean to my *mamm*. He made her cry."

Lizbeth thought her heart would break as a tear rolled down Benuel's cheek and then another. "But Jonah is gone now and Ishmael will come no more," she assured him in a firm voice. She smiled toward Fredrik, taking in the glint of red in his hair, his sweet smile. "Your *daed* will make sure of that. You need never think about Ohio again."

The child leaned back against Fredrik and sighed, as if the weight of the world had been lifted off his chest. "It's *gut, ya, mamm*? I have a real father."

A peace came over her unlike any she'd ever felt before. "*Ich ish gut,* Benuel. We are a family at last."

Benuel moved his leg back and forth, his face relaxed into a hopeful smile. "Can I have a *bruder* now that I have a real father? I've always wanted a *bruder* to play with."

Fredrik looked Lizbeth's way, his eyes searching. She'd told him about her *sohs* who had died, their lives cut short by the abuse she'd endured from Jonah. Could she have more children? Only *Gott* knew that answer, but Fredrik had said he was fine with one child or many. "If it is *Gott*'s will, you will have a *bruder* and maybe a *schweschder*, too."

"I'd like a *bruder* more," Benuel admitted with a smile and then squirmed down off his father's legs and ran around the churchyard, his energy suppressed far too long.

"He took the news well," Fredrik said and hugged her close, his lips coming down on hers in a warm kiss. "Now let's get something to eat before my belly has a say in all that matters. The hour grows late."

Arm in arm the newlyweds walked back into the church, their son at their side. Life often took many sharp twists and turns, but *Gott*'s will was finally done.

* * * * *

*If you enjoyed
HER SECRET AMISH CHILD,
look for these other Love Inspired titles
by Cheryl Williford.*

**THE AMISH WIDOW'S SECRET
THE AMISH MIDWIFE'S COURTSHIP**

*Find more great reads at
www.LoveInspired.com*

Dear Reader,

Thank you for returning to the quaint little Amish tourist town of Pinecraft, Florida, and investing yourself in the lives of Lizbeth Mullet, Chicken John's widowed daughter, and Fredrik Lapp, Mose Fischer's newest furniture builder and salesperson. God revealed this fantastic young couple's past to me as I wrote my first two Pinecraft books, *The Amish Widow's Secret* and *The Amish Midwife's Courtship*. What a treat it was to unwind the strings of the past that bind these two hearts together in love. I'd appreciate hearing from those of you who enjoyed reading the story as much as I enjoyed writing it. Contact me at: cheryl.williford@att.net.

Cheryl Williford

Get 2 Free Books,
Plus 2 Free Gifts—
just for trying the Reader Service!

Get 2 Free Books,
Plus 2 Free Gifts—
just for trying the Reader Service!

◆ HARLEQUIN®

HEARTWARMING™

HWI7